Hard Times in Red Grape

*Secrets in small town
California are hard to keep…*

DONNA BARKLEY FLEMING

CCB Publishing
British Columbia, Canada

Hard Times in Red Grape:
Secrets in Small Town California Are Hard to Keep

Copyright ©2014 by Donna Barkley Fleming
ISBN-13 978-1-77143-187-3
First Edition

Library and Archives Canada Cataloguing in Publication
Fleming, Donna Barkley, 1947-, author
Hard times in Red Grape : secrets in small town California are hard to keep
/ by Donna Barkley Fleming. -- First edition.
Issued in print and electronic formats.
ISBN 978-1-77143-187-3 (pbk.).--ISBN 978-1-77143-188-0 (pdf)
Additional cataloguing data available from Library and Archives Canada

Key words: Couples, Suburbia, Drought, Corruption, Water Contamination,
Fracking, Over Development, Secrets, Foster Children, Homeless, Murder

Cover design by Tatiana Villa (villatat@gmail.com)

Publisher: CCB Publishing
             British Columbia, Canada
             www.ccbpublishing.com

ACKNOWLEDGMENTS

I would like to thank Sherry and Sam Steffanoff for their patience in reading my manuscript over and over again. Their suggestions for making my characters stronger were right on. Thank you.

*

I would also like to thank my proof editor Mike Smirnov for his patience in catching all of my mistakes in grammar, tense and punctuation. He helped me to tell the tale in the voice of all the characters who live in Red Grape. "Donna, Bravo! You managed to combine a really good story into a topical alarm about this state's water crisis! Mike Smirnov."

*

A special thanks to my dear friend Sandra, gone to soon; it was Sandra who opened my eyes to the life of children placed into the foster care system. Sandra revealed the daily life of a foster child; never feeling as if she belonged; afraid to speak out lest she be moved again. Sandra felt the pain of no bedtime rituals, no dance lessons, no encouragement. She received food, shelter and clothing and often something more. .

*

During the writing process I often found myself staring at blank pages. I thank my AVHS Alumni friend, and author Michael Gonzalez who encouraged me to stay focused and continue writing.

*

And last, thank you Michael Ellis. He was an inspiration to every life he touched, including mine.

Thank you

Thank you to my mom and dad. My dad was the most ethical man I have ever known. He told us the way to succeed was to be the best at anything. A job as a bank teller, a boat builder, or the president of the United States all deserved the best we had to give. My mom told me to use my creativity and to sit up straight and hold my shoulders back. I was very lucky.

INTRODUCTION

Red Grape exists only in my mind. Any similarity to characters I have known, is a serendipitous fluke; much like an intricate necklace left on a park bench; someone left it in the spirit of generosity. Enjoy each character as if they were a friend just waiting for you to sit down and say hello.

*

Written by California author, Donna Barkley Fleming, who takes her characters from life in suburbia.

Brad and Helen live in small town America just outside of Napa, California. They face increasingly hard times with rising water rates, drought, over development, heavy traffic, and a city council bent on approving all new development. Brad suspects that Helen is playing around while he works as a CPA; and Helen, his lovely wife, writes a cooking blog, but seldom cooks, well, not in their kitchen at least.

CHAPTER ONE

It is a truth known only to married men that while not always in a state of bliss, they are generally satisfied with the comfort of walking into their well-ordered homes at the end of a long day. Thoughts of office politics, gridlock traffic and the escalating cost of living, slip away the closer they get to their familiar off ramps. Crawling down local streets, with their seemingly endless road excavation; that will presumably someday ease traffic in the small town of Red Grape, but maybe not, as new developments are routinely approved by the city. The smell of something, Ahh--is it meatloaf? Conjured or real, the smell of his favorite meal makes any fault of Brad's wife of seven years, fade away. All that is good about Helen comes to mind as he smells the heady meatloaf bubbling in a rich and tangy barbecue sauce, Helen can really cook when she wants to! Her overspending at the mall and the many dinners of takeout food all forgotten. Yes, he is leading a comfortable life in the small suburban town of Red Grape. Named for the abundance of local vineyards, the town of Red Grape is on a fast track to becoming a trendy town like Carmel. Red Grape has the kind of charm that draws weekend tourists to wine tasting events, cozy bed and breakfasts, restaurants with outdoor dining and shopping in charming little boutiques. One shop sells one of a kind, locally designed scarves. Brad recalled the day Helen came home with her eighty dollar scarf. Helen gushed over the water color print that was an original design. "Just imagine, Red Grape has the most artistic, unique, silk scarf shop in America!" Rationalized Helen. Brad let it go and tried to bring back the smell of meatloaf. He could almost smell it that tomato sweetened with brown sugar; a scent lingering in his memory. His olfactory senses were working overtime, connecting his emotional memory to the times when he had come home to meatloaf. Brad hit the garage door opener and pulled into the driveway of his small suburban home. Grabbing his suit jacket and tie, he stepped out of his SUV. One long stride and he stooped to grab *The Grape Leaf*, a local paper covering their small community in Napa, California. Headlines read, "Drink Wine, Not Water!" Brad walked through the garage and into the house. On entering the house he smelled.... nothing, unless you counted the smell of burnt coffee; obviously the pot was left on all day. Brad turned toward the front door to see something strange. The front door knob was on the floor near the front door. He thought of his wife. Nothing smelled like dinner cooking. He called to Helen. "Helen are you here?" No answer. Then the doorbell rang and Brad walked to the front door with the knob still in his hand.

"Hi Brad!" said Kate, their neighbor with a passion for cats, and rumored to have at least 20 felines constantly coming and going. "Have you heard that Red Grape is being forced to ration water?"

Brad looked down at *The Grape Leaf.*

"Is that what these headlines are about?" Brad asked. Kate with her bright red hair and bright blue eye shadow, leaned in closer to look at the paper.

"Yes, I guess it is. I just received my water bill which is up again in March, when it's usually down. This water issue is getting out of control. Did you and Helen get your water bill?"

Brad remembered writing his last check for his water bill for over one hundred dollars. "Yes, Kate, but I have the actual bill at my office. I remember thinking it was high."

"We need to do something," implored Kate. "I talked to Cynthia and she said her bill was over two hundred dollars! Now they are asking us to ration water?"

Brad interrupted Kate on her rant and said, "Have you seen Helen?" Just then a cat sauntered up the front walk and Kate stooped to pick up the huge tabby. The animal must have weighed thirty pounds.

"No not today, I thought she was here. Well I have to run; talk to Helen and maybe we should attend the city council meeting next week together. Water is on the agenda!"

Brad agreed and watched as the cat lady lugged her big tabby across the street. Another day in suburbia: a broken door knob, high water bills, no dinner, and no wife, mused Brad. Still standing at the open door as the sun was setting, Brad started to look into what had happened to the broken door knob. Just then, Helen rounded the corner of their street.

Brad watched Helen, in a pair of tan capris and a blue sweatshirt come walking briskly down the tree lined street. Her blond hair, cut in a sharp blunt line, doing that swish, swish, thing and even at thirty-five, she looked great. She could probably still belt out the school cheer from twenty years ago. He had fallen in love with her as she cheered her heart out in their Napa high school pep rallies.

> *Who's got spirit?*
> *We've got spirit!*
> *Freshmen stand up, let us hear it!*
> *Freshmen rock, there's no doubt about it,*
> *If you don't believe us, stand up and shout it!*

Helen still bounced like a cheerleader. She was the typical American girl next door and she never lacked for energy. "Sorry," she called as she waved to Brad.

"Honey it is six thirty, the door is broken." He handed her the door knob. "And you did not cook…again." Emphasis on again…

"Pizza or Chinese?" said Helen as she set the door knob down on the kitchen counter like it was unworthy trash. "Nothing lasts anymore; I'll pick up a new set this week."

Brad was remembering the imagined smell of meatloaf and feeling pissed, mentally cursing his over active olfactory memory. After working all day, take-out was not what he had in mind.

"I was hoping more for meatloaf; where have you been?"

"Mrs. Daly fell and I went to help."

Brad just gave her the look; the one that was supposed to say, "Do you think I am stupid?" Lips tight, eyes direct, all knowing.

Helen had learned to ignore "the look", she knew he did it to make her feel small and, not in a good way. Writing a cooking blog was not exactly the career or life she had planned. By changing the subject she avoided a conflict. Problem handled. Brad handed her, *The Grape Leaf*, proclaiming "Drink Wine, Not Water!"

"Great idea!" said Helen. "Red or White?"

Brad took a deep breath and gave in again. "Red," said Brad. Helen stood on her toes and gave her tall husband a kiss on the cheek, just short of his mouth, and breezed past him into the house.

"Do you want to check the take-out list?" asked Helen.

"Who has meatloaf and mashed potatoes?"

Helen paused to think. "How about meatloaf tomorrow?" said Helen with that cute tilt of her head, as if the tilt made a question without using words.

"Or spaghetti?" she said with that beautiful smile. Those beautiful white teeth, so girl next door. And, Brad had paid ten thousand dollars in dental bills to make that smile perfect. Brad liked perfection. Again he pushed these thoughts away and started looking for the red wine he wanted from the wine rack. Brad was pouring them both a glass of Road Side Red Zinfandel. "So how is Mrs. Daly? She has fallen, what…three times now?"

Helen had the menu from *Spaghetini* in her hand and was reaching for her cell phone.

"Okay…how about spaghetti and meatballs?"

Brad nodded and Helen already had her cell in hand. Brad turned on the news and brooded over his lost meatloaf. The television was tuned to a local news station and a reporter was rambling on about the drought and water rationing in California.

Brad sipped the rich dark red zinfandel, and savored the black current flavor that was like comfort in a glass. As they sat waiting for the take-out to arrive, Brad asked about the broken door knob.

"It has been loose for a while. I think it must have fallen off when I ran out of here."

"Why, Helen, must you always be the one to run over to help Mrs. Daly?" Brad complained, as he continued to sip the rich red wine and wait for food. Helen tilted her head and said, "I must be on their speed dial, I always get the call." Brad shrugged and the doorbell rang. Take out had arrived. Helen went into action getting the dinner served. "You know they need help from time to time, he is eighty and she may be too, but she won't tell anyone how old she is. That is one of the many secrets in this neighborhood, how old are the Daly's, when will they sell their home? Carol Marcel's husband died while jogging of unknown causes. And, how many cats does Kate have?" Rolling her eyes she sipped the rich red wine. "Secrets in suburbia," murmured Helen.

Brad said, "Kate was here by the way, about the water bill, and she thinks we should all show up at the city council meeting." Suddenly Helen choked on her wine. When she composed herself, she blurted, "Why would we do that?"

"Well, to complain about the water rates, and ask why the city council always approves new developments regardless of water supply and ignores the traffic buildup, I guess."

"Brad, you know I hate to talk in public!"

"It seemed to me that Kate was ready to give the city council a ration. So, she probably just wants community support," Brad explained.

"Well, she better be careful. I heard the city gets tough with people who complain about anything. She will suddenly have someone serving her with some permit violation about all of those cats she keeps in cages in her garage," Helen said.

"Oh, true! Now I am sure that is why she wants us all to be there. But the more I think about it, I think we should go to hear what the mayor has to say about the water bills, the drought and the continued new building approvals. Some towns in California have a moratorium on building homes or pools during this drought. And, it took me thirty minutes to get through town today," Brad responded testily. Helen was clearly not interested in attending the city council meeting, so she ignored Brad's complaints.

"Well, I am going to take a shower; hopefully, we still have hot water. What do they mean by conserve?"

"Take a shorter shower," Brad said.

Helen ran up the stairs and Brad heard the water go on. He

would never completely understand the woman. He had hoped they would have a child, but it had never happened. Trying to relax, Brad picked up his latest James Patterson book. Hmm, he was just getting to the part where a woman's sailboat was in trouble on the high seas. At the last minute, her husband had business and couldn't join the family outing. Yep…thought Brad, a husband who had come home to an empty house and no meatloaf had revolted. He could see where this thriller was going. Brad planned to attend the city council meeting. Hopefully, tomorrow there would be meatloaf.

CHAPTER TWO

Helen's Secret

Helen turned on the shower, then grabbed her lap top on the way back to the bathroom.

She had always intended to contact her old boyfriend Rusty, though there never seemed to be an appropriate time; and after today, she knew she would have to take steps to keep her secret in her past. She had no idea that Rusty would ever show up in Red Grape. It was by chance that she called a handyman to repair the broken doorknob and she was shocked to see Rusty standing at the front door, a man she never thought to see again. Rusty was just as surprised to see Helen. A woman he had loved once upon a time. Now he had shown up at her front door. She had opened the door to see the tall muscular guy wearing a light blue tee shirt, with those smiling blue eyes, holding a note book. They had talked the afternoon away. Now, she had only moments to get a note off to Rusty. His business card said, "Waters Construction, Serving Red Grape" with an e-mail address. Now she could get a message to him.

Helen's email read: *Dear Rusty, Please do not come to the house again. By now, I have been married for seven years; so our past is best left in the past. My husband does not know what happened while he was away at college. Please let it go. Helen.*

Closing the lap top, Helen jumped in the shower and was drying off as she heard Brad come up to their bedroom. As she dried off, she searched for a place in the bathroom to stash the laptop. She put it under the bathroom sink, planning to retrieve it later as Brad slept. She grabbed her night shirt and pulled it over her head before leaving the bathroom.

"Did you save me any water?" said Brad teasingly.

"It was still hot when I finished, Brad, you are kidding right?"

said Helen. "That we shall see," mumbled Brad, ambling and stretching as he walked toward the shower. "I do not believe there really is a water shortage," declared Helen as Brad turned away. "Kate seems to over react and she is such a gossip. I would not put too much stock in her alarming news."

"Water bills over one hundred dollars a month is news Helen," said Brad, "and I am glad to attend the city council meeting to see what is going on in our quiet little suburban town."

Helen decided not to reply; but let sleeping dogs lie at this moment.

Suddenly, Helen hiccupped, a thing she did when she was nervous. She knew it would not stop and could go on for an hour.

Having finished his shower, Brad walked into the bedroom buck naked to grab his boxers. Brad's head came up as he noticed the bed moving and his wife sitting with a book, the lamp on, and Helen hiccupping. "God Helen, you know I cannot sleep with you hiccupping for an hour."

"I do not hiccup for my own amusement," replied Helen irritably.

"When is the next city council meeting, Brad?"

"Next Thursday night."

"Then, Helen, you may have the advantage over all of your many neighbors like the Daly's, as I intend to get the real scoop on these high water bills. And, with luck I can talk directly to Beau Geyser after the meeting."

"Really Brad, how can you allow yourself to get involved in all of this city council gossip?"

"You never know, I might learn something. I look forward to meeting some of the regulars who attend those meetings. You don't need to attend, I'll make your excuses to Kate, and I will take our city government participation on myself."

Helen stared at Brad as he got into bed and turned over. Helen hiccupped and tried to relax. She sensed Brad was about to complain again. Throwing back the covers, Helen went down to the kitchen to make some lavender and honey tea. It always calmed her. No wonder she was nervous. She had been so shocked to see Rusty standing at her front door; it had been eight years! She had suggested they meet in the park to talk. She told him where to meet her. She and Rusty had lost track of time. Hiccups no wonder; lucky she did not have a heart attack. She had been lonely with Brad away at college for four long years. Since Brad needed to take summer classes too she had not seen Brad for four years. She and Brad communicated by phone and letters all through college, but she never mentioned Rusty or her life in Napa while he was away at school. Rusty was a nice guy, and never made Helen feel dumb. But when she had become pregnant, she had to deal with a problem she had never expected. Helen sipped her tea pondering the problems she had back then. She and Brad had planned out their whole life when they were in high school. She would work and attend the junior college in Napa while he attended the University in Washington. They planned to have two children after they bought their first house. Brad did well as an accountant in Napa, and within a year they were able to qualify for and buy their first house in Red Grape. Helen had gone off the pill and had been trying to get pregnant for five years. It had never happened. She knew he wanted a child. How could she ever tell Brad that she had given a child away? The fact that she had become pregnant while he was away at college would destroy their marriage. Her hiccups had finally stopped. She made a note on a pad in the kitchen: defrost ground beef for meatloaf. Quietly she walked upstairs, listened for Brad's shallow breathing, and walked into the bathroom to retrieve her lap top and set it on her desk, ready for her cooking blog tomorrow. Tomorrow she would write the new recipe for chicken breasts stuffed with spinach and goat cheese, a side dish of broiled tomatoes to go with it. She would have to suggest a wine. Which vineyard had sent her a bottle of wine lately? One of the perks of writing a cooking blog in Napa was the occasional free bottle of wine for mentioning a vineyard. Tomorrow she would use Road Side Vineyard: perfect!

CHAPTER THREE

Brad Attends the Red Grape City Council Meeting

Brad was among the earliest to show up at the city council meeting the following Thursday evening. He had intended to do a little handshaking before the meeting started but that did not work out due to an unscheduled private meeting of the council members behind closed doors prior to the public meeting. Brad wondered what the city council could be discussing in a private meeting. Helen could not be talked into attending the public meeting, claiming her cooking blog deadline was tomorrow. Brad assured her she would not have to speak in public. What was going on in Red Grape? And who, if anyone, was uncomfortable meeting him face to face? Helen had begged off attending the city council meeting, as he suspected she would. For some reason she did not want to mingle with people lately. Helen used to be so social, but, she was becoming a recluse. A year ago, they attended city events, fund raisers, and restaurants regularly. Something had changed. Helen's entire world had become spending time only with the neighbors and her sister Sherry. Another reason, to give Brad doubt, as to who else his wife spent time with during his long days at the office. Could she be involved with that sleazy city council man, Conally, who was the head of two nonprofit organizations in town? Pat Conally had certainly slobbered all over Helen at the last town picnic. Now that Brad recalled the incident Helen had seemed disgusted by Pat, who had a reputation for spending more time at the race track than behind his desk selling insurance. Helen was devoted to writing her cooking blog. She never showed any interest in city government or in horse races for that matter. Still, Brad wondered. Or, perhaps his wife really did spend hours helping, elderly neighbors, friends in crisis, and strays. He idly wondered if Helen filled some internal mothering need, since they had never been able to have children. Observing his neighbor Kate seated in front of him with her bright red hair pulled back in a knot, he waited for the council members to file in and take their seats.

"I hope Mr. Geyser will explain the hike in water billing, Kate," Bead whispered.

Kate turned in her seat to say "hello" and continued. "We are not likely to get the truth from him, since he voted to raise the water rates," said Kate quietly. "Did they all vote for the water rate increase or just a majority?" asked Brad. "It is always the same three who vote as one," said Kate. Those flashing blue eyes accented by lots of blue eye shadow made her a woman hard to ignore. Kate was a widow and loved pets, a regular Doris Day for animal rights. Brad had to give her points for showing up at these meetings. So many people just complain about the state of affairs but, do nothing.

"If possible Kate," said Brad, "can you introduce me to Beau Geyser after the meeting tonight?"

"I do not believe Beau Geyser will hang around for introductions. They say he is having an affair and his wife does not know. But, of course she does know. Poor woman, I guess she likes being the mayor's wife, and pays no attention to his little flings. But, I never gossip."

"Nor I," said Brad; "I am glad you are planning to speak on the water issue. We all appreciate your effort, Kate." The rugged man seated next to Brad smiled.

A tall man with a cowboy hat sat quietly listening to Kate's run down of the community taking seats. Mister tall, dark and handsome wore work jeans, clearly worked with his hands for a living and judging by his overly tanned face and arms clearly spent a good deal of time outside. Women loved his type. Brad took an instant dislike to him. Kate waved at someone else coming in as she said, "that is Stormy Johnson, she writes for, *The Grape Leaf*. She wrote that recent expose about the eighty thousand dollars in campaign donations from contractors and developers to our mayor. She is supposed to be some sort of a journalistic investigator." The woman looked like a child of the 80's generation. "She often says her parents were hippies during the sixty's. They named her Storm."

Brad directed Kate to the council members filing in. All eyes turned to the council member and mayor as they filed into the seats at the front of the city hall. Mayor Geyser wore his self-importance like a suit of armor. The others seemed to be nothing but followers. The pledge of allegiance was called and all stood. Next, Mayor Geyser called for oral comments. When Kate's name was called, she walked to the podium. She clearly announced her name and began to complain about the increased cost of water in Red Grape. The mayor appeared uninterested. Mayor Geyser appeared to be gazing into some place or someone behind Kate. Perhaps he was just bored. At three minutes Mayor Geyser said, "Your time is up. Thank you for your comments." The next order of business was announced. A new group of village homes were scheduled to break ground with final approval going to Robbers Development. Allen Robbers came to the podium to assure one and all that they had completed the traffic study. There would be no adverse environmental impact to the planned community of two hundred new homes that would be built on the site of an old vineyard that had gone out of business. The mayor called for a vote. Three of the council members said yea, and two nay. "Passed!" said the mayor and down slammed the gavel in Beau Geyer's hand. Brad watched as he saw the future of Red Grape That had just acquired two hundred more families, who would need water, utilities, and they would each own two cars adding to the ever increasing traffic snarls. No wonder the developers donate to Beau Geyser; the guy is a crook in a suit.

CHAPTER FOUR

The Night of the Red Moon

Helen had called her sister Sherry. When things got bad, Sherry was the voice of reason. It was time to talk to her sister. Sherry drove over from Napa. It was April and the night was beautiful. The moon was full and red, it seemed to glow. Helen had made a large pot of lavender honey tea. She considered her favorite port, but knew Sherry would decline. Sherry, the forever sensible sibling in her family, had big brown eyes and a long soft brown pony tail. She looked the same as she did in high school. Sherry was married to a prince of a man who actually cooked for her. She had married young and her children were grown. Brad greeted Sherry on his way out the door to the city council meeting. When Helen and Sherry were alone Helen knew she had to drop the bomb and get her secret off her chest. Oddly, it was the night of the red moon and magic was in the air! Before tonight, Helen had told no one about her former life and what had happened during that time nine years ago. Her family thought she had traveled to Europe. In reality, she had moved to a small town in central California. No one knew her in Corralitos. At the time, Sherry had been in Grant City, Illinois, taking care of their ailing and aging grandmother. Brad was away at college in Washington State. Ten years ago, she found herself with tough decisions to make. The first thing Helen did was to go to the book store. She wandered through the rows of books on child birth, abortion, raising a child as a single mother and giving a child up for adoption. This is the way Helen approached any crisis, research. She approached the register with her stack of books feeling as if the checker could read her mind. This was one decision she needed to make without family interference. Helen drove down the coast and stopped in Corralitos for lunch. Corralitos was a small town and Helen found a bed and breakfast with an available room. She checked in with her overnight bags and books. The woman who owned the B & B offered her tea, and Helen sat in a cozy window seat in her tiny bedroom reading the day and night away. It felt odd but comfortable to be at a B & B alone. Helen took a long walk to the harbor the next day and stopped for clam chowder at a quaint fisherman's restaurant on the small pier. She never felt alone if she had a book. Thinking of all the jobs she had since leaving high school, Helen remembered her position as office manager for a sign company. She thought back to the day when her boss had given her instructions to fire a young woman in the office pool. The woman's name was Esperanza, which means hope in Spanish. Esperanza was a single mom and was often late to work. She either had child care problems, or her child was sick and she could not be in that day. Helen explained this to her boss, Richard, who was an old fashioned guy who demanded his employees be on time and ready to work each morning at eight am. It was Helen's job to let the young woman go. She never forgot the horrible experience. Helen felt worse than Esperanza that sad day. Now she looked at her future, and the future of her unborn child. What was best for everyone? Rusty was not ready to be a dad. He was even then off on a fishing boat in Alaska. No, she would have to give the child up. She researched private adoptions. This would be the hardest thing she would ever do. It was not the pregnancy that bothered her, it was the finality of handing over her child to two strangers. As long as she could review their background, she felt this was a good thing to do for her child and a blessing to parents unable to conceive. When she returned from the overnight at the Bed and Breakfast, Helen poured out her heart to her sister Sherry. She felt then and now that Kids need two parents.

Sherry was astounded that Helen had gone through a nine month pregnancy and handed over a baby to a family without saying anything to her own family.

"Rusty just wasn't what I wanted in a husband," said Helen. "Sweet, good hearted, but also aimless, and with no ambition; but, he was an honorable man." Helen showed Sherry a picture of

Rusty.

"He is also handsome," replied Sherry, "which is not a bad thing, and if he had a good heart, you had a rare man, yet you married Brad, why?" Sherry looked at Helen with tears in her eyes. Helen reached for the bottle of Grignolino Port with a touch of orange; she poured a small shot into her tea. Helen sipped her tea. It had been a time to decide which way to go in life. Had she told Brad the truth he would have gone off with some college girl; Helen knew that.

"I felt like I was standing at a fork in the road. Remember that poem; *two roads diverged in a wood?* Well, I had to choose a road. It was a cross roads in my life. Yes, I was attracted to Rusty by all of his attention to me; he made me feel intelligent, sexy, worthy; he was great for my self-esteem. It was all just fun. Then I got the call from my doctor's office."

"Did Rusty ask you to marry him?"

"Yes he did, but Brad and I had already planned out our lives together. We planned to marry when he graduated from University. Our lives together had been plotted out since high school graduation."

"I remember," said Sherry, "but people change. How do you feel now, and, why are you just telling me now? Somewhere out there I have a niece or nephew," Sherry added.

"That is one of the reasons I did not involve family. I had to make this decision alone. I wanted to be sure my child had a solid, two parent family. She would be nine years old by now."

Sherry grabbed the port and poured a bit in her tea. "You have to be careful, Helen, because I think your cross roads are turning into the Bermuda Triangle. So how did you run into Rusty again?"

Helen sipped her tea. The port warmed her. The combination of lavender tea and port flavored with oranges was giving her courage and calm at the same time. She needed to write about this in one of her cooking blogs.

"Well last week the door knob broke. I called a handyman listed in the local *Grape Leaf* directory. Rusty showed up at my door last Tuesday with his tool box. He was as shocked as I was.

Looking just as tall and handsome as he ever did; he lives in Red Grape now. He has started a business, and he is getting his life together. I met him at the park and we talked for two hours."

"Of course he wanted to know how things had turned out with the delivery. Had the attorney worked things out with the couple, and where was Rusty while you were pregnant and working in a book shop in Podunk?"

"Off to Alaska to work on a fishing boat."

"Oh God!" exclaimed Sherry, "Like those guys on television?"

"Yes, just like that. He knew someone in Alaska who was willing to take him on and he promised to send me money during the pregnancy."

"And, did he?"

"Yes, he sure did. He sent me a fat check, along with a few lines on a post card every few months, when he was not out fishing on the Bearing Sea."

"He was a good man to make sure you were okay," said Sherry.

"Yes, we parted well. I assumed he was still in Alaska, possibly even married by now."

"Well he sounds like a decent guy who I hope will not disrupt your life."

"All people are good in your eyes, Sherry. I never heard you speak badly of anyone in your life," Sherry responded,

"I always give people a chance; but I always say what I think."

"I know you do; and *that* is what makes you the perfect sister. You were blessed with good sense, our mother said it often," said Helen as she sipped her tea. "Yes, I have a daughter and you have a niece out there in the world. I arranged for a private adoption through an attorney in Napa. Rusty knew this attorney, Mr. McReady, and a great family that was willing to pay all of my medical expenses. Everyone thought I was off to Europe. Actually, I was in Corralitos working at a funky little book shop. Some trip to Europe huh?"

Sherry listened in silence, but was not convinced that Helen had done the right thing; her marriage to Brad had not been perfect. But, what marriage was?

"So I guess that means it is not your fault that you and Brad have never had a child?"

"No, but Brad doesn't know that." He has always assumed it was my fault that we couldn't have kids. How can I tell him that I know I can conceive, because I have had a child?"

"You know Brad, he likes perfection. If we couldn't conceive the normal way, we would just live our lives as the happy couple who had no children."

"So have you communicated anymore with Rusty?" Sherry asked.

"I did…I sent him an e-mail asking him not to contact me again, and to leave our past, in the past," Helen said.

"Well, do you trust him?"

"Yes, I do; I do not think he would make trouble for me."

Sherry asked, "So why are you so scared?

"Well," Helen paused. "The lawyer who arranged for the private adoption, Mr. McReady." Helen took another sip of tea and port. "McReady is now living in Red Grape, and he is one of our city council members."

"Oh no, said Sherry. Does he remember you?"

"I don't think so, but I avoid the city council meetings. My last name is different. I was almost introduced to him at a local picnic and when I saw him I escaped to the ladies room about the same time Pat Conally started to drool over me."

"Who is Pat Conally?" Sherry asked.

"Pat is one more creep who is on the city council. He sells insurance as a profession, and spends a lot of time at the horse races. He also drinks too much and has money problems."

"Brad wanted me to go to the city council meeting with him tonight about this water crisis."

Sherry had started to enjoy her tea and port. "Well, there is going to be a hot time in Red Grape if this news gets out."

Helen replied, "Of course, there is the attorney client privacy thing, but he could blunder when he realizes that he handled an adoption for me. All I need is a blunder in front of Brad."

Just then, the garage lights went on at the front of the house.

Brad was home from the city council meeting.

Sherry looked at her watch. "Nine-thirty I better get going. Just remember I am a phone call away."

"Thanks for listening Sherry." They toasted with tea cups and Sherry greeted Brad as he was coming in.

"How was the meeting, Brad?" Sherry asked.

Brad shook his head. "Our mayor is a crook and the city is permitting two hundred more homes just two miles from our little piece of heaven."

Brad and Helen walked Sherry to her car. The moon was glowing red. April fifteenth· some kind of super moon, a time of for changes. Brad put his arm around Helen and they watched as Sherry drove away.

"Have we got any of that meatloaf left? I am so hungry."

"We do," said Helen. Nothing like food, to change the subject.

CHAPTER FIVE

Big Money Influences Red Grape

Just across the street from Brad and Helen on Brandywine Lane lived Kate Summers, a widow woman who had devoted her life to rescuing unwanted pets. She had thirty cats in her home most of the time. She kept the garage door down to avoid being observed by passing neighbors and nosy city inspectors. She cleaned the cages regularly, and hosed out her garage every day. Brad and Helen had become very friendly with their eccentric neighbor, and Kate in turn would hate to see anything disturb Brad and Helen's seemingly perfect family. It was sad that Kate had never been able to have children, but it happens. Her kitties had become like her children and she took the responsibility of caring for each one seriously. Her animals were all well cared for; she rescued strays and found homes for hundreds of cats every year. Still, Kate kept a low profile where the city was concerned. She watched who came and went on their street, so, she could not help but notice the tall handyman getting out of the blue pick-up truck parked in front of Helen's house a couple of weeks ago. Later, she saw Kate go for a run. Oddly, the tall man had left just moments after arriving. Odd, that was the same day Kate had gone over to talk to Brad about the water rates. He seemed to think Helen was missing. Probably nothing, and Kate had bigger fish to fry. That bottom feeder of a mayor was gonna get caught. And, Kate intended to bait the hook.

Red Grape had its problems, and Kate considered that those problems originated with the city council, especially the mayor. Beau Geyser had arrived ten years ago, and had been elected and re-elected for the last eight years. Having attended the city council meeting again tonight, she brought her notes to her computer and started her weekly editorial, tying the mayor to serious corruption.

She had taken the precaution of using the pen name of Sunny Day. Kate pulled up her last post:

Big Money Influences Red Grape
By Sunny Day

Contributions to the mayor's re-election exceed ninety thousand dollars.

Mayor Geyser's job is to advocate for the residents of Red Grape, which he does not do. The mayor and Mr. McReady are politicians through and through. It's a shame that these elected officials are more concerned with serving themselves than being servants of the people. I haven't seen this much ducking, dodging, and weaving since Mohammad Ali's last title fight! Are residents of Red Grape really supposed to believe that ninety thousand dollars were raised to get Mayor Geyser re-elected to this five thousand dollar a year job? And, Mr. Geyser campaigns on the promise of lowering water rates but continually votes to increase water rates once in office. People need to know that contributions are coming in from developers, realtors, oil companies, and contractors. Developers and corporations that need council approval for re-zoning to develop new homes are very grateful. The owners of these new homes will buy new cars, and the developments all need water. Wake up residents of Red Grape!

The campaign contributions used to re-elect Beau Geyser and his team, were turning Red Grape into a money making machine. Kate paused to reflect on what she knew about Beau Geyser. He had a wife named Barbara with whom Kate was particularly friendly. Though not even Barb Geyser knew that Kate wrote the weekly column for *The* Grape *Leaf.* Her editorial position at the local paper required anonymity. Covering issues in the small town with the inflated water bills, runaway development and ninety thousand dollars in campaign contributions for the last re-election of Beau Geyser required caution and anonymity. To compound problems, there was the odd death of John Marcel. John was a water conservation expert who had been found dead on the side of a jogging trail that wound through an abandoned vineyard. John Marcel and his wife, Carol, had moved to Red Grape just last year. John had been hired by the Red Grape water department to evaluate the feasibility of pumping additional ground water from the town's main aquifer, a move that was supposed to increase water production and thereby reduce water rates. Something about groundwater fracking and its negative effects on water quality had been in a preliminary report. Shortly thereafter, John went for a jog one morning and dropped dead. The town officials were calling it a heart attack, yet the man was only fifty five and in seemingly good health. Well, heart attacks did happen suddenly. Kate would like to think the mayor was somehow responsible, but that was just too evil, even for Beau Geyser. During a recent lunch with the mayor's wife Barb, at the Jug of Wine Eatery, Barb and Kate chatted about the recent events in Red Grape over French onion soup and crusty bread. Everyone was talking about the drought in California and the water shortage was becoming impossible to ignore. Kate was eager to hear from Barb about Beau's new girlfriend. His wife Barb had been a beauty contest winner back in her day. She was still a striking woman. Her grey hair was a clever Audrey Hepburn cut and with her pearls and dark glasses she was often mistaken for a movie star. Barb was the perfect wife for a mayor. Her image gave Beau credibility. Barb took a sip of her glass of red table wine and shook her head. "He will never stop wandering. I have given up fighting with him about his little affairs. Let him do it. As long as he keeps me in silk scarves and is reasonably discreet I just do not care anymore."

Kate grabbed her old friend's hand. "I am so sorry he has turned out to be such a jerk Barb, at least you have your children raised and a grandchild on the way. Happy news, right?" said Kate.

Barb smiled at her old friend Kate, but Barb looked sad. Kate sat quietly and listened as Barb talked on about how Mr. McReady had formerly struggled as an attorney in Napa, making a barely tolerable income writing wills and arranging private adoptions, a service that was profitable, but rarely requested. Most women just used abortion to solve the problem of an untimely pregnancy. "Such a shame when childless parents are willing and eager to pay thousands of dollars for a private adoption," said Barb.

According to Barb, Beau had convinced, McReady to move his little legal practice to Red Grape, a growing community that could use his services. McReady readily accepted the advice and had become the right hand of Mayor Geyser. McReady now sat on the city council as legal advisor and was compensated by the town of Red Grape when, and if, the mayor was ever challenged on water rates or land acquisitions. The recent purchase of a bankrupted vineyard, drawing up of a land contract, the property's sale and the vineyard's re-zoning as a planned community were all handled by Mr. McReady and by Carol Marcel, who had wasted no time in getting her California Real Estate license after moving to Red Grape. Carol had been appointed head of the Open Space Foundation and worked closely with the city council on matters related to land sales, rezoning and acquisitions for the city. The developers had been very grateful. After McReady had closed his practice in Napa, he had moved with his family to an upscale condominium about a mile from downtown Red Grape, where he could think with pleasure of his own importance. A big man in a small town, he posed as a kindly barrister, quite different from Beau Geyser, who was known for his ruthlessness. Yet, McReady's business flourished and he was grateful to Beau for the steady work flow and hefty legal fees flowing into his bank account. He charmed everyone; everyone but Kate, who wanted to expose the graft in Red Grape.

Suddenly, Bully, her thirty pound Tabby jumped in her lap. "Oh my, who wants attention? Let's get a snack shall we?" Kate left her keyboard and headed to the kitchen to feed Bully. She needed to check on her other kitties too. There were not enough hours in the day, mused Kate. She smiled as Bully daintily nibbled his kibble. She opened the refrigerator and stared inside. "Ahh, a carton of flan, just what I need for a midnight snack." Kate talked to Bully as if he were just another close friend. Bully ignored her and then followed her up the stairs and jumped on his favorite spot near the end of Kate's bed. Kate finished her snack and turned out the light. It had been a long day.

CHAPTER SIX

Rusty Is Listening

Rusty was the quiet observer seated next to Brad Elson at the Red Grape City council meeting. On hearing the exchange between Brad and Kate before the council assembled Rusty picked up enough clues to know that Brad was Helen's husband.

Rusty had intended to meet contractors and pass out his business card. It was no secret that Red Grape was building one development after another. He had hoped to land a contract with a developer to grow his business. It seemed clear to Rusty that these developers were connected and their projects were being passed on through by that self-important little man, Beau Geyser. He had quite a little scam going.

The city council meeting broke up at about nine-thirty. Rusty watched as Beau hurried to his assigned parking spot, slither into his silver Beamer and headed into town. Rusty decided to follow him out of curiosity.

Rusty had been thinking about Helen for several years. He knew she did not marry him nine years ago because he was flighty and had no life plan. He understood. But, he had never been able to forget the child that they had. He had a daughter living with her adopted family somewhere in Napa. He wondered what she looked like. She would be nine year old. He prayed she was with a good family.

Rusty was so happy to see Helen. He hoped she was happy. But, for some reason he doubted it. She seemed nervous when they talked in the park. The night after their chat in the park he had later received an e-mail from Helen asking him to put the past, in the past. She made it clear she wanted to keep Rusty away from her home. He understood. But, now that McReady was living in Red Grape he suspected trouble was ahead for Helen. Perhaps, that is why he followed Beau. Driving at a safe distance, Rusty watched as Beau parked his Beamer in the Chit Chat Inn parking lot. This was the only local pub open past ten o-clock in Red Grape. Rusty parked and walked in five minutes after Beau. Beau was in a dark booth in the back of the Chit Chat, talking to a blond woman. They appeared to be arguing about something. Rusty sat at the bar and ordered a Blue Moon. Bar tenders were full of information and the gal behind the bar was not immune to Rusty's good looks and easy charm.

Sally, the bartender, said, "You just passing through our small town or did you come for the wine tasting?"

Rusty smiled that killer smile, "No, I moved to Red Grape about three months ago. I heard the construction business was good here."

"So you're a contractor then?" Smiled Sally, as she leaned closer to Rusty.

Rusty took a long pull on his Blue Moon. "Yep, business was slow in Napa."

Voices were escalating in the rear booth, and both Rusty and Sally turned to see an angry blond woman, who had been waiting for a table for an hour, become a bit animated.

Sally shook her head. "Sounds like our mayor's latest little fling is giving him trouble."

Rusty and Sally both heard the raised voices coming from the back booth.

The woman said, "You think you are so important, you with all of your little side deals. How many condos and homes do you own now, Beau? Ten, twelve and what about the land with the oil well? I suppose you think I am going quietly into the night while you retire to the Bahamas. You have been getting one house with every new development you pass through the city council. You told me your wife was crazy. That was just a lie to get my sympathy, and you know it, Beau. Everyone speaks well of Barbara. I was so stupid to trust you!"

Beau's right hand whipped out at Anna across the table like a snake, and clinched Anna's wrist. Her wine glass flew with a crash to the floor, and the contents of the glass sprayed Anna's coral sweater. Anna yelped in pain and shock. In one smooth move, Sally grabbed a hidden baseball bat and rounded the bar with the grace of a ballet dancer. "Beau you asshole, let go of that woman NOW, or your hand will never lift another gavel. I get real testy when I see a man hurt a woman. You may be the mayor or Red Grape, but in this bar, I call the shots. Let go of that girl! What your wife sees in you is a mystery to me!" Beau let go of Anna slowly and taking out his wallet, threw down a hundred dollar bill and said, "Let's just say this never happened, okay Sally?" Sally was cleaning up the broken glass as she kept an eye on him. Beau was half way out of his seat, leaning across the table, again threatening the blond when Sally stepped up with the baseball bat, poised and ready to swing. Beau's threat was so intensely chilling that Sally was frozen momentarily in place. As a bartender, she had heard this all before. She hissed, "Beau, it's water under the bridge unless I hear that anything happens to this young woman. I am sure that nice young man at the bar can dial 911 if you touch her again. Are we clear?" As they all turned to look at Rusty, the man at the bar had the phone in his hand. "Sure Sally," Beau said, just a misunderstanding. "You are fine, right Anna?" Anna was sniffling and holding her wrist. "Let me get some ice for that wrist," Beau said softly. "She is fine," Sally snarled. "Beau you and I go way back; she needs ice and I'm getting it now. You can keep your big tip, I see you touch a woman in my bar again and your name will be in the paper." '*Mayor attacks young girlfriend in the Chit Chat Inn.*' "Wouldn't your voters just love those headlines?" As she turned to get the ice, Sally heard Beau Geyser's threat directed at her. "I heard you were serving beer to under age patrons and I am sure Jordan Loggs was a witness, so be careful, Sally." Sally whirled around and said, "Listen to me, you fucking jerk! I don't know how you became mayor, but we have security cameras in this bar. I think I will save tonight's tape. And, if you serve me with any of your stupid code violations, that tape is going to the sheriff and the newspaper. You got it, pal?" "Now Sally calm down, Anna and I were just leaving. No need for more of a row.

Just a little tiff; no harm done." "Right, sure, that's why her wrist is swelling." "And, just so you know, I would call your wife about this if she wasn't such a classy lady." Then Sally turned to Anna, "Honey, he ain't worth it. Move on. He will only cause you grief." Anna smiled shyly at Sally, and then got up to leave with Beau.

As the couple walked toward the front door, Sally and Rusty heard Beau telling his girlfriend about her secrets and how lucky she was for his protection.

"We all have secrets Anna, and anytime you want to move out of that condo I pay for in Bella Vista, sweetie, that condo that I own, you just go right ahead! You are replaceable, you know. Move on back to Napa and keep selling junk at the Salvation Army to all your homeless friends. With luck, you can set up housekeeping under the freeway overpass like some of your friends. Did you like that life so much?"

Anna started to cry. Sally felt so sorry for the woman. Normally she ignored Beau's relationships with his femme fatales, but this one seemed so vulnerable. She knew Beau was using her just as he had used a long string of women. Rusty watched as the couple left the Chit Chat together. "That gal will have a swollen wrist tomorrow, bet on it," said Rusty.

Sally returned to the bar, clearly rattled, and returned her attention to Rusty. Rusty was nursing his beer. "So, are they regulars?" asked Rusty.

"Yea, they are," Sally said as she replaced the baseball bat under the bar and she tried to shake off that chilling experience. "Our mayor manages to keep both a wife and a girlfriend. He is a piece of work!"

"Never a dull moment huh?" Rusty said, tipping his glass.

"Man you said it. You'd be surprised what I hear and see as the bartender here at the Chit Chat."

"For instance?" said Rusty. Sally leaned across the bar. She was clearly interested in Rusty. "Well, we have the early birds who come in for their two for one drinks around six pm. They drink and complain. Later we get the couples who are married and sneaking out, much like Beau tonight. And he is not the only one. Bored housewives, using guy's bad business deals turned into love affairs. I have seen and heard it all. Then, later, the hard core drinkers come in. I have had to use this bat a time or two to get their attention. Then, there are the business men in suits who meet to celebrate their latest big deals. Amazing what goes on in this small town of only thirty thousand residents."

"Thirty thousand and one," quipped Rusty.

They laughed. Rusty paid for his beer and said, "See you again."

"Sally," she filled in the blank. "Good night!" With a tilt of her head, and a cute smile. Rusty filled in his name, "Rusty! If you ever need a contractor?" He left his business card on the bar, smiled, and walked out into the April night. Such a charming little town, with all those smart little shops and quaint little downtown bistros; it is all too perfect, he thought. He walked to his truck and thought of all the hidden lives just under the surface of this quiet little California town. He had intended to steer clear of Helen, but he needed to tell her what he had found out about McReady and Beau Geyser. Sally would be a good source of information about who is doing what and with whom in Red Grape. Alaska had been calm compared to Red Grape, California! The night was quiet, and the moon was a big red ball. Leaning against his truck under the big red April moon, Rusty's heart ached as he thought of his daughter. He had yet to tell Helen that he planned to send a long letter to their daughter. Such a quiet town for so many secrets, he thought.

CHAPTER SEVEN

Dear Daughter

It was with apprehension that Rusty dropped the letter to their daughter into the mailbox. He could finally not live with himself thinking that possibly he was needed by his daughter, and so the letter was mailed. It said:

April 13, 2014
My dear daughter,

I know this letter may come as a surprise. It will be up to your mom to give you this letter when, and if, she feels the time is right. Dear daughter, it is not for lack of love that your mother and I arranged for an adoptive family. Your mother was very young. We were very much in love, but she was more adult than I was back then. She knew I was not husband and father material in those days. I was running from one adventure to another. We both agreed on one thing; we wanted the best life for you. We were both very immature. If you can find it in your heart to forgive me one day, I would very much like to meet you. Please know that you were, and are, loved by two people who are just now not in your life. I imagine you having my blue eyes and your mother's blond hair. There may come a time in your life when you will want to meet your biological dad. For this reason, I am sending this letter to your mother. She will know when, and if, the time is right to pass this letter on to you. I have been all over the country but always come back here. I felt the need to be near you and to be sure you were safe. I have kept track of you. I recently watched you on the tennis court at Vintage High School. You have a great serve! I am so proud of you. You have your mother's blond hair and her beautiful smile.

Little one, I want to tell you how sorry I am for not being the father that drives you to those matches, that coaches you, and who helps you with your homework. It is my loss not to be in your life. So I am writing this letter to tell you that I love you. I wish I could be in your life, but I will not upset your family by disrupting your stable family. All seems very well with you. There may come a day when you need me for some reason. Even if you are just curious about meeting me, never hesitate to contact me. Nothing would make me happier than to get a call from my little girl. I will always be rooting for you. You are just as beautiful as your mother. At the time I am writing this letter, you are nine years old. I can be reached at the address below.

You will always have a place in my heart.

In the end, little one, if you stumble and need a hand, please grab mine. I have a business in Red Grape, and I am as close as the phone.

Your first dad,
Rusty Waters

CHAPTER EIGHT

Helen Is Cooking

Friday morning and Helen was trying to focus on her cooking blog. Brad left the house early. With her latte and her lap top in hand, Helen tried to stay focused on her cooking blog. Today she needed to think about comfort food. Croque monsieur might put her in a better mood.

Recipes from Chez Helen

A traditional French croque monsieur sandwich is usually dipped into eggs then grilled on a sandwich-grilling iron. In my kitchen, Chez Helen, I serve this traditional French sandwich on healthy country oat bread from our local bakery, La Bou, in Red Grape. With the added decadence of a creamy cheese port sauce, your husband will be eating out of your hand. Serve sandwiches with a hearty red zinfandel from Road Side Vineyard– Enjoy, food lovers!

Helen finished her blog and posted it to her site, *What's Cooking at Chez Helen's?*

At that moment her cell phone started to play, *"La Vie en Rose."*

"Hello," said Helen.

"Hi Helen, can you talk?" asked Rusty.

"Rusty, hi, I am so sorry for that brief message the other night. I know it sounded blunt considering our history together."

"That's fine, Helen, I get it. You have a new life. I don't want to mess things up for you, I just wanted to give you a heads up."

"What?" said Helen?

"I attended the city council meeting last night."

Helen drew in a deep breath, waiting for the bomb. "Uh oh."

"You got it. As luck would have it, your husband sat next to me."

"Oh God!" said Helen. "Did he speak to you?"

"No, I gather Brad would look down on a man like me, a man who works with his hands. He was chatting with one of your neighbors named Kate."

"Yes, she lives across the street and keeps about twenty cats," said Helen.

"She was a wealth of knowledge about who's who in Red Grape."

"I'll bet she was! She is a wise old woman; red hair and bright blue eye shadow aside, nothing escapes her in our small town."

"I think the old babe is on to something, Helen."

"Really, you mean like, more than high water bills?"

"Well, that is just the tip of the ice berg. When I moved here, I heard it was a growing town. I had no idea why all the development was booming here when the rest of the California is in a recession."

"So, what do you think is going on? Brad said our mayor is a crook in a suit."

"Brad is probably right and that's not all. Mr. McReady was sitting to his left, and he is a member of your city council, the lawyer who handled the adoption, remember?"

"I know," said Helen. "I have been nervous ever since the last community picnic when I almost stumbled into him. I have been avoiding the city council crowd ever since."

"Did McReady recognize you?" asked Helen, apprehension in her voice.

"No, it has been ten years, and I don't think he would recognize me. You spent more time with him than I did when you were drawing up those private adoption forms."

Helen paused. She hated to remember that time.

"Rusty, I am so frightened. My sister was here, and I finally told her what I had done. Sherry thinks my 'decision at the crossroads' is leading me to a Bermuda Triangle." "You know, a place where all your past decisions collide and glug, glug, glug."

"She could be right, Helen. I saw Beau Geyser in action tonight. I followed him after the city council meeting," Rusty said.

"Really, where did he go?"

"Our slick mayor stopped in at that little bar, the Chit Chat Inn down town, and being the curious type, I went in for a beer. He was meeting a young blond, and she was half in the bag when he got there."

"Wow that is sad, but not surprising. I had heard rumors, mostly from Kate, but I never really saw him with anyone else, and this is such a small town."

"Well, it turns out Beau owns a little condo in The Bella Vista community, just outside of town, I got the impression that Beau Geyser is keeping that little blond in his condo. The girl looked to be about twenty-five to me. She was giving him a hard time. Voices got loud and the girl mentioned the many properties that Beau has acquired using his position as the mayor. The waitress and I watched as he got a little rough with her. You know me; I was about 20 seconds from tossing that old guy across the room. Fortunately, the bar tender handled it. That sweet gal runs a tight ship and she has a low tolerance for men abusing women in her place."

"That would have been Sally," Helen mused.

"Yes, and Helen, the Mayor is one man I would not want to cross. Steer clear of him, Helen, McReady too, I am pretty sure they are connected in a quid pro quo, kind of way."

"Thanks Rusty, let me know if my name comes up, but do not tell anyone you know me."

"You got it, babe. Now do you want me drop off that new door hardware?

"Oh, I have to deal with that, but I'm not sure how to replace it and pay you."

"Helen, it will take me less than twenty minutes. Just tell me when I can install it. No bill, babe. Can't you tell Brad a neighbor kid installed it for you?"

"Maybe," responded Helen.

"I will figure out a time and I'll get back to you."

"Okay, take care."

"Take care, Rusty." Helen felt like she was being rescued by Rusty once again. Somehow she felt safer. Rusty tucked the brass door set on the floor of his truck and got on with his day.

CHAPTER NINE

Anna Wakes Up in Pain

Friday morning, Anna woke up in pain. Her right wrist was swollen to twice its normal size, and it was purple. She stumbled to the kitchen for an ice pack, frozen peas would work, and made coffee with her left hand. Her whole body hurt; she had rug burns on her elbow and on the side of her face. In a burst of anger, Beau had shoved her across the room as they had entered her condo the night before. He had been deadly silent in the car. She expected Beau would head for the bedroom and expect the usual quick sex and be off to his wife. Contrary to his normal sweaty lust, last night he was angry. On entering the condo, she turned to ask if he wanted a glass of wine. Beau's response was rage. "You have had enough wine," said Beau through clenched jaws. And before she could respond, she found herself thrown across the room. Anna screamed in pain as she landed on her wrist to break her fall. Beau walked over to help her up. "You know better than to draw attention to us when we are out in public. I am the mayor of this town." Anna gasped, "I know Beau, but you said you would meet me at eight-thirty. I had been sipping wine for an hour while you were at the city council meeting." Beau walked Anna to the bedroom as Anna started crying. Beau had apparently realized he could have seriously injured the girl. "Never mind our plans for tonight. Get some sleep and I will call you tomorrow." And with that he was gone. Anna got undressed and fell asleep without icing her wrist. Now her wrist was throbbing and swollen twice its normal size. She needed to go to the medical center. This would be the third time in six months that she needed medical help. The on-staff social worker had asked too many questions the last time, but now her wrist could be broken. She sure couldn't ask Beau to bring her, not after his outburst last night. She loved this little one

39

bedroom condo on the outskirts of Red Grape. Beau Geyser had set her up in the condo six months ago. So far, Beau had paid the utility bills and he owned this little condo outright. One of the perks of being mayor and working with developers was his cooperation in exchange for ownership of a small condo or house in each new development. Beau collected properties as if he were playing monopoly. This was not Boardwalk, but it was not on Baltic Avenue either. She had never lived in a more beautiful home. She had furnished it herself with used furnishings. She sat at the little round kitchen table she picked up at a local consignment shop; two white wicker chairs with red cushions and a small glass top table that was perfect for the small dining area off the kitchen. After all, she had no guests but Beau Geyser. She gazed out of the slider at her view of one of the local gorgeous vineyards. The condo community of Bella Vista was new and had been built on land that was once planted in grape vines. A smooth real estate transaction, some re-zoning from agricultural to residential, and a developer broke ground on a two hundred unit condo community backing up to another prosperous vineyard, complete with a pool, spa, bike trail and a work-out room. Beau was certainly getting rich collecting properties. She sipped her coffee with her left hand, resting her right wrist on a bag of frozen peas. When had it all gone so wrong?

Beau had been so sweet when she first met him at the South Napa Community Shelter. He was older than she and played the concerned fatherly type. As a foster child she had experience with lots of fatherly type men. One of the reasons she and Joe had married so young was to escape from a family whose father had started coming on to her. She had been sixteen when Don Jones had insisted she sit on his lap after dinner. His wife Velma Jones was a pleasant woman who was over worked, with four small children. She attended bible meeting's at the First Presbyterian Church every Tuesday evening. Anna had only been with this family for a few months when Don insisted Anna sit on his lap after Velma left for church. Don made her feel dirty. But, since she was in high school, Anna knew if she complained to Velma or to the school counselor, it meant moving to another family. So she endured Don and his touching and groping hands on Tuesday nights. When Anna met Joe in her art class, they were sitting on the floor working on a joint art project. Anna and Joe started meeting at the lunch tables every day at Napa Valley high school and Anna told Joe what was happening to her in her home. Joe got angry and wanted Anna to talk to the school counselor, but Anna knew better than to make waves. She remembered their conversations like it was yesterday.

"Joe, if I complain, if I say anything, they will pull me out and send me to another home, another city, and another school. I am sick of moving."

"But Anna, eventually he will do more than just touch you," whispered Joe.

"I know, but I need to graduate from high school, and, I have moved four times in about five years. I hate moving and never feeling like I belong anywhere."

"You need to get out of there," said Joe.

"I can hang on, Joe. I've been helping Velma with the cooking and the kids; I stick close to her, and the only time I am alone is on Tuesday nights."

"I have a plan," Joe said.

"My dad thinks I am wasting my time in high school. He said he wants me to join the Navy when I turn seventeen. They have a training program, and I can become a plumber or an electrician and finish my education in the Navy."

"You mean you would leave high school?" asked Anna, looking worried. Joe had always been her closest friend at Napa Valley High School.

"Yes, and don't freak out, but this is my plan." Joe went on to describe his plan for them both.

"If we get married, there will be base housing for us."

"Oh, Joe. That is wonderful. But, I have to finish high school."

"I am looking into it, Anna, but I know you can finish at night school. At least it will get you out of that house and away from that wacko guy. Did you ask Velma about going to the junior prom yet?"

"Yes," she said. She was not sure that they could afford to buy her a prom dress.

"What size do you wear, Anna? I bet you could barrow one of my sister's dresses."

"Really, you think she would let me?"

"Mary? Sure she would. Just get the okay from Velma. Tell her you need to come over and try on dresses on Tuesday night and I will pick you up after dinner."

"Great idea," said Anna. "I never thought I would get to go to a dance like a prom."

Velma had given in. Don was not happy about it, but finally agreed, as long as it did not cost them anything, she could go to the dance.

Anna and Joe had been able to go to the Napa Valley High School prom before Joe left school to join the Navy. Those prom pictures were in her storage shed. When Joe had finished basic training, he and Anna were married in a small service at the First Presbyterian church of Napa. Anna and Joe had been transferred to the Naval Base in Ventura County. They had a tiny little place assigned to them by base housing. Anna felt like she was playing house. She learned to cook and started reading domestic books from the base library. She shopped at the commissary, and they were so happy. Then one day, Joe got orders that his ship, the USS San Antonio, was heading to the Eastern Mediterranean Sea. He had no idea how long they would be in the Mediterranean Sea and coastal areas. They had been so very happy during that first year. Anna had fallen into a routine and felt like she belonged. Joe was her family now. There had been no place for Anna to attend continuation school in Pt. Mugu, but she intended to finish.

Joe and Anna decided that it might be best if they take the subsidy the Navy paid them and Anna could move back to Napa and attend night school while Joe was in the Mediterranean. Joe got Anna all moved into a little apartment. Together they picked out a little kitten. Anna signed up for night school and she named the tabby kitten Percy. He was her only company when Joe shipped out. She was lonely while Joe was overseas. Joe had bought a used Honda when he finished basic training, and Anna had learned to drive and now had a driver's license. She was doing well in school, but she had too much time on her hands. Anna took a job at the Salvation Army on Franklin Street in Napa. As a sales clerk, she met lots of homeless people stocking up on clothes and camping items to make it through the winters that could be quite cold and wet, even in Napa, California. Jolene had been on the streets for two years after losing her family. Anna had become friendly with Jolene, and, Anna helped Jolene as much as she could. There was a whole community of homeless people in Napa. Their lives were hard. Mostly, they preferred camping to staying in the shelters, but Anna had allowed Jolene to use her bathroom to shower a couple of times a week. Jolene had lost her parents and had no hope of getting a job looking so scruffy. Eventually, Jolene had become pregnant. This was a problem for homeless women. They were vulnerable. When Anna was notified that Joe had died of a mishap on his ship, she was devastated. Joe was the only family she ever had. And now he was gone. There was a small life insurance policy of ten thousand dollars that she had stashed away, and that helped to ease her pain. Anna lived with her cat Percy, and her only friend was Jolene who was growing by the day. Anna thought that a private adoption might be a way to place the child and to get her medical bills paid. Jolene was distraught. She felt very alone and abandoned. If things had been different, Jolene would have loved this baby, but Anna still had not completed her high school diploma requirements. Raising a child was out of the question. But, she was okay. Anna was just very lonely but Jolene was getting desperate.

The day before Anna turned twenty one, she made an appointment at an upscale beauty salon. She asked for some high lights. She chatted with June, the hairdresser at Jean Michael's salon. June was just a few years older than Anna and had a boyfriend. June mentioned a local jazz club in Napa, and suggested she go in for a drink one night. Anna had never been to a bar alone so she convinced Jolene to come along, it was her twenty first birthday. Anna got dressed in a pair of black slacks and a black sweater, got her courage up and drove over to the club. She also helped Jolene to get dressed for the occasion. Once at the club, Anna ordered a glass of wine and Jolene ordered a coke. Together, they listened to the live band and their singer. Wearing all black and a new layered haircut and blond highlights, Anna looked older than her age and felt pretty.

That was the night Anna met Franco. He had been sitting at the bar and walked over to Anna after she got her drink from the server.

"Can I buy you a drink?"

She lifter her glass and said, "Thanks I am good for now."

"Ah, maybe next time?" Franco said.

Anna smiled politely and sipped her rose wine. She had never been to a jazz club, and the music was smooth, like Franco. The man was Mediterranean, probably; he had dark eyes, dark hair and olive skin, and was about five foot ten, she guessed. He wore a large gold ring on his right hand and a Rolex watch on his left wrist. He was dressed in a jacket and steel grey slacks, and what looked like expensive shoes.

"I am Franco", he said with a bit of an accent, "May I join you?"

Franco was not like anyone she had met before; he was older, maybe thirty, and he smoothly slipped into the club chair next to Anna. Jolene was not impressed.

"Yes, hi, I am Anna, do you come here often?"

Franco was not like anyone she had ever met, and he was older, maybe thirty. A foreign accent and his professional appearance were attractive to Anna. She did not see the signs, but, Jolene did. He sipped coffee and cognac. He was interested in her, he asked her about her life, in detail. In fact, they talked for over an hour. Anna's friend Jolene wanted to go home; her ankles were swelling. With great courtesy, Franco insisted, "Please allow me to get a cab for your friend; it will be no trouble." Jolene gave a sharp discreet "no" signal to Anna, but, Anna was enthralled by this smooth talker. Jolene gave up and accepted the offered ride. "I will see you back at home in a couple of hours, Jo, just take a warm bath and relax. I will be fine." Jolene did not feel comfortable with this arrangement, but she went to the taxi stand to wait for her ride. "Please allow me to take your friend home, I will take good care of her," said Franco. Jolene pulled out her cell phone and snapped a picture of Franco. Franco said, "What are you doing?" "Just making sure I have your photo in case my friend does not arrive home safely tonight." And with that, she ducked into the waiting taxi.

When Franco and Anna were alone, Franco began to ask questions that Anna did not realize were getting increasingly personal. Anna learned little about the nature of Franco's business that night, and when they got to the parking lot, he said, "Oh, damn, my driver is gone." Anna was still not alarmed, a cab was called and Anna took Franco home to her apartment. Anna assumed he was financially stable, he had a driver after all; he said… In truth, he didn't own a car and he had an expired driver's license. Anna offered him a drink anyway, but he asked for coffee instead. Thinking back, Anna now knew that Franco was keeping alert and taking inventory.

Anna was later to learn that Franco had many names, and he was involved in many businesses: one was, "Credit Repair" by issuing EINs or employee identification numbers. This turned out to be a fraudulent procedure used to establish a new credit profile. He also bought and sold cars, registering them in Nevada. Franco was fortyish, but Anna, much younger, didn't care. Anna was falling in love.

As it turned out, Franco, a confidence man, did his homework on Anna, and then he went to work draining her bank accounts, running up credit card debt and even grabbing her life insurance. In the following days, Anna set Franco up in an office leased in her name. He charged designer suits, office furniture, computers and art to her accounts. The business he set up used Anna as the figure head. He even incorporated under her name and bingo, Anna was the president of a corporation she knew nothing about. She was the signatory on a business checking account, but Franco simply took the checks, and signed Anna's name. On one occasion, Franco loaned a client $20,000.00, and signed her name to the check. He continued to lead her along, telling her they were going to make big money together. He discouraged her from allowing Jolene to stay in her apartment any longer, even though Jolene was due to deliver her baby soon. Anna finally convinced Jolene to speak with an attorney who specialized in private adoptions. "Listen," said Anna, "I know this is hard, but you have no job, no family and that baby needs a better life than you can give it right now. I work all day, and I can't help you. Please consider the private adoption. Some of these parents cannot have children and are willing to pay for your medical expenses in exchange for adopting your baby, and I believe you can negotiate something financial for yourself. You need to get an apartment and go back to school, Jolene." Jolene was tearful, but knew Anna made sense. Jolene only wanted the best for her child. "Okay, I will see the attorney, but promise me you will be careful with Franco. He is not the kind of man you can trust." Anna, ignoring her comment about Franco, gave Jolene the business card of Mr. McReady in Napa. The card said, *specializing in private adoptions*. A few days later, Jolene told Anna that she had signed the adoption papers and that she had received an initial check for three thousand dollars. All arrangements had been made by Mr. McReady. Jolene soon moved into a tiny apartment in Napa. This suited Franco fine because he needed to move in with Anna to complete his plans. Jolene promised to stay in touch with Anna. Oddly, that was the last time Anna ever saw Jolene.

Two year later, Anna was no longer so naïve about her love, Franco. Still living in the same small dark apartment in Napa, Anna worried about her mounting bills and credit card debt. The rent hadn't been paid in six months, and the landlord showed up at odd hours screaming at her to get out. Franco continued to string Anna along, but by now he had moved on to another woman in the same apartment complex. The woman, Anna noticed, was wearing a bracelet that had been a gift from Franco to her. Franco had told her he needed to liquidate, for the business. Anna was hurt and angry but Franco kept promising to make good on the mountain of debt. Anna realized that she was soon to be on the street. Then, Anna met Beau Geyser while working at the Napa Salvation Army Store...

CHAPTER TEN

Helen Meets Anna

Helen got through another week without running into any more problems with Brad. She worked on her cooking blog, and cooked numerous dishes of shrimp and green chili quesadillas, with guacamole, for Brad who loved coming home every evening to the exquisite smells coming from the kitchen. Helen passed yet another night trying to rid herself of hiccups. It seemed lately that they came on only when Brad came up to bed.

After sitting in the kitchen for a while, drinking her lavender tea, she idly worked on her cooking blog. By midnight, she was calm enough to go back up to bed. Helen knew that Brad was growing suspicious of her nightly hiccup attacks. She decided that she would go to the local walk-in clinic tomorrow and see if there wasn't something they could suggest to stop this nightly event.

Crawling into bed in the dark, Helen did her best not to disturb Brad. She put her head on the pillow and took a deep breath. Just as she was relaxing, Brad said, "What is going on with you, Helen?" So much for peace. "Just another bout of hiccups, Brad. I do not do this to annoy you, which is why I go down stairs."

"Seems odd!" said Brad. "It never used to happen so often."

"I will go to the doctor and see if there is something they can prescribe," said Helen with cool calm. Brad's lack of sympathy was grating on her.

"I am sure you feel for me, Brad." She added, "Let's try to get some rest before the night is done."

Brad let it go. Helen was different. He knew that for some reason she was sticking close to home. She was avoiding his invitations to dinner at their favorite restaurant, or to the jazz club.

She used to like those places. Something was up, and, he thought it was tied to the city council members, whom Helen avoided for some reason.

The next morning, Brad was up early despite his lack of sleep. Helen woke up groggy, threw on her robe and headed downstairs for coffee. Damn, Brad had taken all of the coffee. He could be so selfish at times. Most times! Helen brewed another pot of strong coffee and went to turn on the irrigation system in the yard. Brad had turned it off after the last high water bill. Helen had to stand at each station for five minutes to be sure that her roses and lavender got a drink.

Back in the kitchen her coffee was waiting. Helen heated some milk in the micro wave, whipped it, and poured in the strong French Roast. Ahh! She was starting to feel human. With her latte in hand, she sat down with her cell and started to call her family doctor, then changed her mind. Helen grabbed the local *"Grape Leaf"* on the table and sat down to look at the advertisements. Sipping coffee and reading the paper she saw the editorial by Stormy Day: *Big Money Influences Red Grape*. There was also a piece about the new development to be built in town. And there below the piece about the new development was a picture of Mayor Geyser, McReady, and a developer named Allen Robbers All three were holding shovels at a ground breaking ceremony. That was too strange. Rusty had been right about McReady being connected with Beau Geyser. No wonder he decided to start up his construction business here in Red Grape. Next, she saw an ad for home repairs and construction services by Rusty Waters. Looking further, Helen found what she was looking for. There, at the bottom of the page was an ad for Red Grape Urgent Care.

Our fees are substantially less than those of your hospital's emergency room. They are even lower than those of an average visit to a doctor's office! There is no appointment necessary. You simply come in any time you need medical care. Our staff will see you in less time than it takes to fill out the "emergency room's" paperwork...

This is what Helen needed, a clinic where she wouldn't have to answer a bunch of questions from her family doctor. Helen called the number listed and was told by the operator that she could just walk in.

Helen grabbed a banana and ran upstairs to take a shower. By ten thirty that morning, she was sitting in the waiting room of Red Grape Urgent Care. Seated next to her was a pretty young blond woman with her wrist in a cast. She was reading, *A Taste of Home, Meals in Minutes.* As Helen also had an interest in food, she said hello. "Hi, I see you are interested in food, I am Helen Elson and I write the local Cooking Blog in town." Anna looked up surprised that anyone would speak to her.

"Hi, I am still learning how to cook. Anna McKinney, nice to meet a celebrity. I am a widow; I was learning how to cook when I was married to my husband, Joe," said Anna in a rush. "Really?" remarked Helen. "You are so young to be a widow."

"I know; it sure came as a shock to me. My husband was in the Navy and he was killed in the Mediterranean."

"I am so sorry!" said Helen. Helen looked down at the cast on Anna's wrist. "Did you fall?" For some reason, Anna seemed nervous.

"Yes, silly really, just one of those freak things," said Anna.

"Well, feel free to check out my blog sometime."

"I will," said Anna. Just then, the nurse called Anna into the examining room. Helen had finished filling out her paperwork and gave it to the nurse. The nurse put Anna in an examining room and came back for Helen. "Might as well get you both back; the doctor will be with you soon."

As Helen sat in the examining room, she mentally composed her concern regarding her nightly hiccups. Stress was her self-diagnosis, yet she wondered what the doctor would say. The walls were thin, and she suddenly heard the doctor's deep, foreign accented voice in the next room.

"Anna, you have been here three times with these accidents.

We become concerned when we see so many falls in one patient. You were lucky again. This was a very bad sprain with possible ligament damage. Have you been taking the anti-inflammatory medications we prescribed after your last incident?" She could not hear Anna's response. "Do you have any friends in town whom you could stay with, Anna?" asked the doctor. "I know you are new to town; and have you found a job yet?"

"No, I haven't!" said Anna. That was loud enough for Helen to hear. Her heart went out to this young girl. She seemed so alone, and something was up with all those injuries. Helen pulled out her day timer and scribbled a note on the 'To Do' page. *Anna, call me if you want to have lunch one day,* she scribbled, *Helen Elson,* along with her address and phone number. Helen folded the note in half and stepped toward the opening examining room door.

"Anna, here is that recipe I told you about," and she handed Anna the note with a smile. Anna said, "Thank you," wondering what recipe Helen could have meant and left the facility with a new wrap on her wrist and with a prescription for pain. Helen hoped Anna would call her. What was one more neighbor to look after? She enjoyed looking out for the Daly couple, and this young woman also clearly needed a friend; probably an abusive boyfriend, she mused. Her thoughts were interrupted as a doctor named Lynn walked in.

"Hello Helen, how can I help you today?"

Helen explained that she had been having hiccups recently in the evenings, and that they often disturbed her husband. Doctor Lynn asked about Helen's stomach, and any changes to her diet, to rule out a gastrointestinal disorder, and then he asked her about spicy food.

"No on all counts," replied Helen.

"Honestly, they seem to come on when I am nervous." Dr. Lynn said, "Sometimes, persistent hiccups occur without a rational cause, and these are known as idiopathic chronic hiccups. Before we start more tests may I suggest some warm calming tea?" Helen explained that she had tried this and in fact, the hiccups always stopped with the warm tea. "Any chance you could be pregnant?"

asked Dr. Lynn.

"No, I have pretty much given up on that. I have been married for over eight years and no baby," said Helen. "Well, I think you have this under control. I could prescribe muscle relaxants, but honestly they can make you drowsy, and I think your hiccups are brought on by stress," said Dr. Lynn. As an afterthought, Dr. Lynn said, "Well, I keep hoping for some new mothers in Red Grape, but we have not seen many. Never have I worked in a community with so few new mothers!"

"Really said Helen?" As Helen left the clinic she remembered the doctor's words about so few new mothers in Red Grape. Helen wondered why that could be. Water, everyone was talking about water. Maybe the water was affecting the health of the town's residents, maybe even something related to sperm count, a subject she did not want to broach with Brad.

Helen left with no prescription, just a handwritten note recommending a cup of chamomile tea at bedtime. As Helen started her car, the CD player rotated to "Coal Miner's Daughter." Helen listened to the old familiar lyrics with Loretta Lynn's familiar cry in her voice. Helen remembered her own dad who passed away several years ago. One of her favorite memories was when she was about 13 years old waltzing with her father in the family room of their small home in Napa. Actually, it was not her first dance lesson, but definitely the most memorable. Although her mother had enrolled Helen in tap, ballet and ballroom dancing, she learned how to dance from her father. The waltz lessons from her father consisted of Helen in stockings standing on her father's feet, arms in position, and waltzing around the family room. He was a beautiful dancer. Her dad grew up in the sixties and had learned to dance from his older sister, Ruth. When Helen was attending her first, boy-girl dance, she remembered the waltz. Her dad held the perfect form and moved with head high, shoulders back, and moved his legs in long gliding steps. Helen wondered if her daughter would ever know that kind of love. She hoped so. Suddenly, she realized she was crying.

Helen was again struck that she had no children to teach to

how to dance, to cook, to write, or to read stories to and to tuck into bed at night. What special gifts did her little girl have that she had given away? She paused and remembered Dr. Lynn's comments about no new mothers in Red Grape. Why was that? She looked out at the sidewalks and noticed the couples walking and lingering in outdoor cafés but where were the children of Red Grape.? No mom's and strollers anywhere. They had been everywhere in Napa, mom's with expensive jogging strollers were everywhere. She suddenly realized that there was not one new mom in her community, at least, not that she knew. That was truly odd!

The following day, Helen stopped at the grocery store and picked up ground beef for taco cobbler. The recipe called for ground beef, melted cheddar and salsa. To Brad, this bubbly golden cobbler was heaven on earth. Not her usual sophisticated kind of dish but who cared. Keep the guy happy. But what would make Brad really happy was - a baby. Well, it was not because they had not tried.

CHAPTER ELEVEN

Anna Spills the Beans on Beau Geyser

On getting home in her old Honda, Anna went up to her little condo in Bella Vista. The place was still sparse, but she loved the beautiful view and the charming little area. Beau arrived around eight in the evening, and used his key as usual, as if he owned her along with the condo. He walked into the kitchen as Anna was reading a recipe and trying to prepare something with her left hand. But, his eyes settled on the cast on her right wrist. "Was that necessary, Anna?" said Beau. "I have torn ligaments, Beau. Sorry." "But you know I have a reputation to maintain here in town, you cannot just run off to the clinic for every little bruise." Beau had come over, after dinner with his wife, having given her some excuse about a business meeting. He did not expect to see Anna wearing a cast and with rug burns on her face. He did not insist on sex that evening, and Anna was grateful. Beau questioned Anna about her conversation with the doctor, and Anna told him she had been discreet, but that the doctor had been asking lots of questions about the injury. Beau was always concerned about gossip, but much less concerned about how Anna was feeling. "So, how did you pay for the medical visit?" asked Beau.

"Every time before, they have been billing me." Beau asked to see the bill. To date, Anna's Urgent Care bills amounted to $1900.00, and she had used his condo as the billing address. This tied Anna to Beau through medical records. "I'll take care of this," said Beau as he put the bill in his wallet. "There have been prescriptions too, Beau. Fifty dollars a week living expenses does not go very far. If you will just let me get a job, I can earn my own money," said Anna. "No! That was our original agreement, Anna. I will remind you if you do not remember: I said you could live rent free in my condo and I would pay the utilities and all other bills.

Considering that you let yourself be taken in by that Euro trash Franco, the guy who took all your money, ran up your credit cards, and squatted in your apartment, I'd say it was a good trade off. You obviously need a keeper!" Beau put his hands on his lapels and rolled back on his heels as if he were a man of great importance. "You are lucky I rescued you, Anna," Beau lectured. Anna did not feel lucky. She did not need a keeper, she felt trapped. Anna had made one of those decisions to run when she couldn't get rid of Franco. Now she was trapped with a fifty- five year old man who was the mayor or Red Grape; not a nice guy, a guy who lived by quid pro quo. He did nothing for anyone without payback of some sort. Anna loved this little condo in Red Grape, but it did not belong to her. She was living like a prisoner! Anna was so very lonely, and once again felt isolated. She had traded her freedom for a lovely condo, but she was getting angry about the entire sordid arrangement. Anna knew she needed to finish school in a hurry and get a job.

Beau did not want Anna mingling with the populace of Red Grape. Beau handed Anna two one-hundred dollar bills to keep her from complaining any more about her condition. Beau provided just enough money to feed her, but not enough to do anything more. Anna was still getting a stipend from her late husband's navy wives allowance. That money went into her bank account in Napa. At least she had been smart enough not to mention that to Beau. If Beau knew about it, he would take the money and she knew it. Just like Franco, he would insist that he had just the right investments for dumb little her and he would manage the money for her, just as Franco had done before Beau. Beau left within an hour. Good bye and thank God, thought Anna. She put the two hundred dollars in her purse and then she saw the note from Helen. She intended to call Helen tomorrow, and the following day Helen received a phone call from Anna McKinney.

After some brief arrangements, Helen and Anna arranged to meet downtown to shop and to have lunch. Anna was so excited about spending time with a woman friend, even though she knew this was against Beau's "house" rules. But she needed to talk to another woman!

Helen and Anna spent next morning's hours wandering through the town's consignment stores, and ended up at a cute little side walk café for lunch.

Helen was cautious when talking to Anna, but she did want to help her. She felt sure that something was very wrong in this woman's life, and, Anna seemed so very alone.

"Whatever made you decide to move to Red Grape?" asked Helen; "Since you were in school, didn't you have friends in Napa? This is a family community and you are so young, and single."

"I should have stayed with friends in Napa," said Anna. "You must have guessed by now that I came because of a man?" said Anna.

"Oh! Yes—I understand your situation perfectly."

Helen remembered her life twelve years ago. She had been lonely while Brad was away at college. That was when Rusty came into her life.

"I wish I could tell you that all will be well. Sometimes you just have to make a decision and go with it, even though it may not be a comfortable decision. About ten years ago I had to make one of those 'cross roads of life' decisions."

"Helen, it seems that I have been moving all of my life. I was a foster child, so I got bounced around often. I love this little town of Red Grape and I had hoped to make a fresh start here."

"Well, you still can," said Helen.

Anna took a deep breath and felt a leap of faith in the woman sitting across from her.

"After I lost Joe, I got a job working for the Salvation Army in Napa. I met a whole group of people that live on the streets. Do you have any idea what those people go through, living on the streets? I was so close to becoming one of those people. An older man came into the Salvation Army store to drop off a donation and he saw me. He asked me to lunch. It seemed harmless at the time. Well, I ended up telling him my story, which included a boyfriend who had invaded my apartment and was living on my sofa, a boyfriend who talked me into investing my entire savings account, which included my life insurance money from Joe. Franco was his name. He also ran up my credit cards, and since then my credit has been ruined. I cannot even rent an apartment."

"Anna," cried Helen, "remember this is the twenty first century! You are free to come and go where you want. Why don't you look for a job here in Red Grape? I have lots of contacts?"

"So where are you living now?" asked Helen.

"That is my big problem, Helen."

"Why?" Helen tilted her head in that question mark tilt of hers.

"I agreed to a bargain with Beau Geyser. He said he owned several vacant properties, and that I could live in one of his condos."

"How very generous," said Helen sarcastically.

"He even agreed to pay for the utilities, in exchange for sex."

"What? What? But, the mayor is married to my friend Barbara and, and... Oh my God Anna, do you know what would happen if this got out?"

"Yes, that is why I cannot get a job or make friends in this town; it was the agreement I made with Beau."

"I had to agree to keep our friendship private," continued Anna, looking embarrassed.

"What? What? Okay! Well, all deals are off, Anna. We will find you another apartment and a job. You cannot be bought and sold. He cannot have that power over you. They outlawed slavery, you know!" Said Helen, whose blood pressure was rising. "That bastard, how could he take advantage of you like that? This kind of thing does not happen in Red Grape. You are the victim in Beau Geyser's little scheme. You are just a young girl!"

"I said yes, Helen. I agreed. If this gets out, I will look like the whore in the relationship."

"Tell me Anna," said Helen, "did Beau Geyser cause the injury to your wrist?"

Anna looked across the table with tears in her eyes. "Yes, and this is not the first time. Beau can be scary; he has a bad temper. He is doing something illegal to acquire all of these properties as

Mayor of Red Grape and if he were to lose his position as mayor and our relationship got out? Well, I think he would kill me to keep things quiet."

Helen drew in a deep breath, leaned back and sipped her ice tea. Something in the back of her mind was niggling through the layers of her memory. Helen closed her eyes and turned her head as if to listen closely. Where had she heard something about murder and Red Grape? Drip, Drip, Drip, water. Helen was silent and thinking.

"We all have secrets Anna," said Helen, and she thought of Rusty. The day Rusty had showed up on her front porch, Brad had asked where she had been. She had been flippant when she remarked about the many secrets in Red Grape. Carol Marcel was a recent widow, John Marcel had died suddenly on a jogging trail, just dropped dead! Hadn't he been hired by the city to evaluate something to do with water supply?

"Anna, did Beau Geyser say anything to you about the properties he acquires. Did he mention any other names?" asked Helen. "A man named McReady perhaps?" "No, but I think he is seeing another woman besides me," Anna replied. "A Carol Marcel. I checked his cell phone and found her number and called her. He had been calling her at odd times. I googled her and she is a realtor who recently moved to Red Grape."

"Anna, Carol Marcel is a widow; her husband died recently."

"Oh God!" said Anna. "I didn't know!"

"Did you speak to her?" Helen asked.

"No, I said I thought I had the wrong number. Her voice sounded distracted. I was just curious about whether Beau had more than one woman he was stringing along."

"Any other interesting numbers when you did that checking?" asked Helen.

"Well, there were several calls to Sun Oil Company, and I noticed some documents in his briefcase from Sun Oil. I have no idea what he is doing with them."

"When do you think Beau will be dropping by your condo?" asked Helen.

"He will probably wait a couple of days. He was alarmed when he saw my wrist in a cast. But he calls. He keeps tabs on me."

"Anna, do you trust me?

"Yes," said Anna, with tears in her eyes.

"Listen to me. We all make mistakes. You have not had the best of luck in life so far. Living within the foster care program was not the best way to grow up. Joe rescued you. That tells me that he was a good man. He died in the service of our country. Now I am not going to let some jerk like Beau Geyser hurt you. He needs to be in jail! Right now, we need to protect you, so, do not tell him you met with me. Promise me, okay?" asked Helen. "Good! Now put my number in a private place. Do not leave your cell phone around for him to see. I have a friend who might be able to help. He helped me once and he is a good man, the best! I know a lot of people here in Red Grape. I am going to dig up some dirt. Just keep Beau in the dark. Do not let on that we," Helen grabbed Anna's left, uninjured hand, "have a plan. "

Anna smiled the biggest smile Helen had ever seen.

"We need to find you a job first thing, and we may have to hide you for a while. Beau is not going to want this business to get out. Number one, he will try to discredit you, but town gossip will likely kill his chances of being re-elected as mayor of Red Grape!"

CHAPTER TWELVE

Helen Is on a Mission.

Helen needed to call her sister, Sherry. She also e-mailed Rusty from her smart phone. It was iffy to talk to Brad about this yet. Helen was still hoping she could keep Brad in the dark about Rusty; the entire problem of the pregnancy, and the adoption so many years ago. No point in involving Brad just yet. She had to get home before Brad and make some calls. Helen did not know Carol Marcel well, but the woman was a new widow. Her fifty five year old husband just died while jogging, and, John Marcel had been working for the Red Grape water department. Water again. Water, Water, Water? It cost too much, people were losing their vineyards, and someone had died while investigating water supply for the town and its ever growing number of developments that depended on it. What is going on in this town? Helen pulled into the driveway of her home. Fishing for her cell phone in her handbag, Helen hit Sherry's number.

CHAPTER THIRTEEN

Helen Dons Her Nancy Drew

In light of what Helen had learned from Anna about Mayor Geyser and his affairs in Red Grape, her own problems seemed small. Helen's nature was to swoop in to help a friend, or a neighbor, but this was like rescuing a town from a corrupt politician who could turn out to be dangerous. Anna's life had been hell compared to Helen's. The consequences of Anna's agreement between herself and Beau Geyser, was akin to signing away one's life as an indentured sex partner in exchange for a free condo. Helen became enraged every time she thought of that dirty old man. For this reason, Helen needed Sherry to keep her cool and to get a plan. Her actions were going to blow the lid off the charming little town of Red Grape, and Helen wanted to get as much information about Beau's business and personal life before she started. Helen thought of Kate and Sally, two very good sources of information; a neighborhood snoop, along with the town bartender. Helen and Sherry arranged to meet the following evening. Anna had heard back from Rusty and he agreed to meet Sherry and Helen the following night. They could not meet at Helen's home, so Helen wrote an e-mail to Rusty asking if they could meet at his house, a small place in town. The small older home had loads of character, but needed lots of work. The landlord was happy to have a contractor living there. Rusty sent a quick e-mail to Helen. *'Helen, I will cook. Plan to see you and Sherry here tomorrow night around seven. My address is 707 Broad Street, just off Vine. See you then, Rusty.'* But Brad, who had planned on being with his wife on Saturday night, would be left in the lurch. Helen and Brad usually went to dinner or a movie on Saturday night. Helen had yet to make an excuse for missing their date. Her mind raced through the excuses for having alternate plans on their Saturday night. She remembered it was "chic flix" night at the local theatre. Sherry wanted to see the latest comedy, *The Other Woman*, which was playing with Michelle Pfeiffer. Brad would not want to see that. To smooth the waters, Helen had picked up the latest Patterson novel, a thriller in a world of genetic engineering and illegal scientific experimentation. *When the Wind Blows* was about human evolution and genetic modification. Brad would love it. She had also thrown together the meatloaf that she knew Brad would kill for. The spicy V8 juice had been stirred into the ground beef, along with oat meal, an egg, chopped onions and into the mold, covered with brown sugar and barbecue sauce, and it was ready to bake for exactly one hour. She shoved it all in the oven at four pm on Saturday afternoon. While sharing a glass of rose with Brad, she passed him the new book she had picked up at the local 'Book Nook'. Brad looked up suspiciously. "Hmmm-- What's up Helen?" and he watched her over the top of his wire rimmed glasses.

"I made plans to spend the evening with Sherry, Brad. Sherry wants to see the movie, *The Other Woman*, and it is playing downtown tonight. This will be my birthday gift to her." Brad picked up the book. *When the Wind Blows* by Patterson and read the cover blurb Genetic *Engineering on Humans*, perfect!

"Okay Helen, go ahead, enjoy your evening with Sherry." The smell of meatloaf was in the air. It was like an aphrodisiac to Brad. The aroma of spicy tomato and sweet brown sugar sauce mingled with beef and onion was making the house smell like heaven to him. Helen knew that Aunt Lorry's recipe had produced the best meatloaf of the Phi Tau Omega women's cook book several years running.

Brad was sipping his wine and browsing through the new Patterson book. "Looks interesting actually. Thank you, and don't think I don't know I am being manipulated." Helen leaned over and kissed Brad on the mouth. "Thanks Brad, and thank you for not making a big deal out of this."

Helen was about to leave the kitchen to get ready to meet Sherry, but stopped. "Brad, remember when you attended the city council meeting and you said Beau Geyser was a crook in a suit?"

"Yes," said Brad. "Have you heard anything more about him?"

"Well, I have been reading those editorials in, *The Grape Leaf*, written under someone's pen name. That person is making some nasty accusations and wants to keep their name a secret. Some back issues have reports on water rates and shortages due to the drought, and I did find a report written by that guy...what was his name?" "Who?" asked Helen. "That new couple who moved here a few months ago; the guy who dropped dead while jogging, what was his name? Apparently, he had written a report about the danger of fracking for additional groundwater supply. John Marcel, remember he had been hired by the city water department. He was some sort of water conservation expert. He basically said that the problem is the amount of water being diverted by fracking and the potential for contamination of the aquifers because of that process. I googled Marcel and he was some very well-known and respected geologist. And, there was that link to The Endocrine Society's report about fracking contamination groundwater quality published last year. It is pretty heavy stuff!"

Helen stopped dead in her tracks. "He writes a report about the danger of water contamination and then he drops dead while jogging. Does that seem odd to you?" "Now Helen, don't let your imagination run away with you. I think Beau Geyser is a crook, but, murder? That is well -- that just doesn't happen in a small town like ours."

"Okay, I will leave my Nancy Drew hat at home. Going up to change to meet Sherry. I should be home by ten and we might get a bite to eat afterwards."

Brad watched his wife run up the stairs. He did not buy her act for a minute. Helen was up to something!

CHAPTER FOURTEEN

Who's Got Enemies?

"I hope, Helen, that you and Sherry like shrimp and chili quesadillas," said Rusty. Helen stood on Rusty's covered porch overgrown with morning glories. "I feel like you are rescuing me again, Rusty. When did you learn to cook?" Sherry was just parking her SUV under the veranda and Rusty and Helen waited for her. Helen waved. "Sherry, Rusty cooked; we will not starve!" "Sherry's husband cooks; he knows how to treat a woman. Sherry, this is Rusty". They moved into the small living room that was furnished with a wide brown leather sofa, a standing lamp and a large wall mounted television. "Excuse the lack of domestic decoration; I have been putting my energies into getting my business off the ground," said Rusty. "It has possibilities, Rusty," said Helen.

"I have heard a lot about *you* from Helen," said Sherry, with the emphasis on the *you*. "I have never known anyone who actually worked on an Alaskan fishing boat. That must have been an adventure!"

"That was a time in my life devoted to adventure. I became a crabber on a fishing boat on the Bering Sea; that is when I learned to cook. But, after one particularly icy cold fishing trip, when we almost went down in bad weather, I collected my check and headed to Montana to work on a ranch. There, I learned the art of fly fishing." "Wow!" said Sherry, "You have really had some adventures!" "Yes Sherry, I was young and I sewed some wild oats, I wanted to live out some dreams before I tied myself down." "Wow, sounds like you accomplished that," said Sherry.

"Let's get this meeting under way. I have much to tell you... both of you," said Helen. "What has inspired you Helen? I thought you wanted to keep a low profile because of McReady," he said.

Rusty poured three frozen margaritas for them and sat them down at the small kitchen table. A bowl of tortilla chips and salsa were waiting. Although Sherry rarely drank, she gladly sipped the icy drink.

"So what changed you mind?" said Sherry. "Do not keep us in suspense."

"Okay, I got angry, really, really, angry!" Rusty and Sherry looked at Helen.

"I went to the clinic in town earlier this week, and while I was sitting in the waiting room, I noticed this young girl with her wrist in a cast. She was reading a cooking magazine so I started a conversation. She seemed remote but friendly. The nurse took her back before me and then she put me in an adjoining room to wait for the doctor. As I sat there, I heard the doctor's conversation through the thin wall. The woman has been there several times for injuries, supposedly because of a fall or accident. He asked her if she had a job in town yet, and I heard her say 'no'!" Rusty was putting two and two together.

"So I quickly jotted down my name and number and went to the door to hand the girl, my note. She seemed surprised, but she put my note in her purse. I thought she might have been a victim of abuse. While we were in the waiting room, she said she was a widow and had moved here from Napa."

"To make a long story short, she called and we met for lunch the next day. This is her story. She was raised within the Foster Care system, dropped out of high school, and married young. Her husband recently died in the Navy. She is the widow of a young man who basically rescued her from a home where she was being abused by the father. But while he was deployed in the Mediterranean, he died. She was left alone in the world at about nineteen. No high school diploma. She was working at the Salvation Army store in Napa and attended night school when some guy latched onto her and offered to help her invest her life insurance money."

Sherry was sipping a margarita and Brad jumped up to throw the quesadillas on the griddle. Helen set the table, and Sherry retrieved the guacamole from the refrigerator. They had become a team!

"This is one of those horror stories that you read about in tabloids," said Sherry.

"It gets worse, much worse." Sherry and Rusty looked at each other. Rusty finally had to satisfy his curiosity.

"Is this young blond by any chance small, blond, with a shaggy hair cut with high lights, about twenty two?" "Yes", said Helen. "Where did you see her, since I gather she does not get out much?"

"Remember that I mentioned to you that I followed Beau Geyser the night after the city council meeting?"

"Yes," said Helen. "I think that is the woman who was waiting for him in the back booth of the Chit Chat Inn," Brad continued.

"Bingo!" said Helen. "Later that night, Beau threw her across the room in her condo. Let me rephrase that. He threw Anna across the room in a condo that he owns and allows Anna to live in; as long as she plays by his rules. Anna is a captive. Beau Geyser is keeping her, paying her rent, after the ex-boyfriend ruined her credit, drained her bank account, and was sleeping on her sofa in Napa. Anna has no one; no one but me now. I won't let her down. Beau offered to rescue her, but, she had to agree to live by his rules, in his condo. Apparently, he owns several properties from some real estate deals he acquired from grateful developers. Beau is also connected to Carol Marcel; her number is on Beau's cell phone. Anna told me that. Anna had to agree to live in his Bella Vista condo and to provide sex whenever he dropped by. Anna just wants to get a job to get on her feet again and he will not allow it. He wants to keep his mistress dependent and a secret. Our mayor is a fifty-five year old sleaze bag in a shiny suit. He does nothing for anyone without a payoff."

"And, Anna is afraid of him." Rusty finally spoke.

"I saw how he treated her at the Chit Chat. He was angry and lunged across the table at her the night I was there. The bar tender said that it had happed before." They all looked at each other. Sherry grabbed her note pad. "Okay what do we know about Beau Geyser?" Sherry started making a list. Rusty spoke and Sherry was furiously scribbling notes."

"Helen how well do you know Kate, your neighbor?"

"Pretty well, she attends those city council meetings. She seems to know everyone in town. She can be a gossip, but, I have never known her to be malicious," said Helen. "I think Kate may be the expose editorial writer, and hiding her identity by using a pen name. She is a wiley old gal!" said Rusty.

"I did ask Brad something before I left the house tonight. I asked if he had heard any more news about Beau Geyser or the city council. Well, Brad has been reading the back issues of the *Grape Leaf*. Apparently, someone is writing editorials under a pen name about Beau Geyser. Also, he mentioned John Marcel." Sherry and Rusty both looked bewildered. "John Marcel moved here to Red Grape to take a job as the water specialist and as a hydrogeologist. He had been employed by the city water department to evaluate whether the ground water system could meet the quantity needs of our ever growing community. John Marcel had also prepared a report on the practice of fracking. The problem is that the amount of water being diverted for fracking and the potential for contamination of the aquifers, which can migrate into the town's main groundwater body." Helen paused to let this information sink in. Rusty said, "We need to talk to this guy". Helen picked up her margarita and leaned back in her chair. Sherry was still taking notes and munching on tortilla chips. "Talking to John Marcel is not possible."

"Why?" said Sherry. "We need to find out what he knows about the water problem and possible contamination. Let's see what else he may know about Beau Geyser." Helen looked at them both. "About a month ago, John Marcel went for a run. He was a jogger. He was found dead on the side of the trail. The cause of death was listed as heart failure. Nevertheless, I think it may be connected to our mayor."

"Whoa!" said Rusty. "I knew the guy was trouble, but murder? Helen we need professional help."

"Why don't we contact reporters who cover investigative journalism? We need, Bob Woodward and Carl Bernstein," said

Rusty. "This is why I called you and Sherry. Our local sheriff is not going to take my suspicions seriously, I write a cooking blog. If we do nothing, Anna is trapped. She has very little money and no credibility. Anna needs a job and a place to live, and she needs to finish school. Anna also knows about the side deals that Beau collects when he approves a zoning change to clear the way for a new developer. Anna could be in danger because Beau Geyser is collecting properties like he was playing monopoly, and Anna knows about that."

"I have a thought," said Sherry. "Why don't we drop in on Carol Marcel? She might know something. Isn't she head of that Land Use group?" Sherry and Helen both turned to look at Rusty. "Okay, mister charm, time to make yourself useful. Rusty, can you drop in on Carol Marcel?" Rusty smiled. Helen gave Rusty a come hither look. "Use your big blue eyes on Carol Marcel." Rusty laughed and said, "Anything for you, babe. I think I need to do a little marketing anyway." "Meanwhile, Sherry and I will try to connect with Kate Summers and find out what more she knows." Helen turned to Sherry, "I think you need a cat."

Rusty made a copy of Sherry's notes and they agreed to meet in a week. Operation Rescue was underway!

CHAPTER FIFTEEN

Something Is Brewing

Brad watched Helen pull out of the drive way with her faux designer tote bag bulging with who knows what. Something was up with more than Sherry's birthday! Brad set the Patterson thriller aside, walked to his office and pulled up his search files on Beau Geyser. As a CPA, Brad knew how to obtain the 461 records of donors who make contributions of $10,000 or more in a calendar year, and independent contributors who make independent donations of $1,000 or more in a calendar year in order to influence local election. Geyser had a long running list of major contributors. Geyser had his very own $10,000 club. Several out of state major developers and one big oil company, Sun Rise Oil, had donated over ten thousand dollars several times over the last few years. His background search turned up a felony assault on Geyser in Napa. Later, the charges were dropped for lack of a witness showing up. A woman, possibly homeless, accused him of rape. The woman, Ellen Cross, accused Beau of rape, and then never showed up for the arraignment. Later, the entire case was dropped for lack of an eye witness, this was in 1995. The entire case was handled by none other than McReady. Well, that is interesting. Brad googled the oil company and found that they had oil wells in Red Grape. The Sun Rise Oil company was listed on the NASDAQ exchange where the company, listed as SRO on the Exchange, had gone from twenty dollars a share in 2008, to forty-two dollars a share in 2014. Well, that is even more interesting. Next, Brad did a property search on Beau Geyser himself. Several properties were listed under the name of the Geyser family trust. What Brad really needed was a copy of Geyser's tax returns. According to the IRS data base, his returns were filed electronically by Jan Geyser, a CPA in Napa, California. Well, obviously he had a relative doing his taxes. Who other than a relative would keep quiet about such misconduct? A man holding a public office with the ability to manipulate zoning changes was in a position to skim lots of cash from grateful developers. Brad sat back in his home office and worried about Helen. What was going on, was she involved?

CHAPTER SIXTEEN

John Goes Missing

Carol and John Marcel were a classy couple in their fifties who had kept pretty much to themselves. Carol had sold real estate in Harrisburg, Pennsylvania before they moved to California. She did well, too. California was a different market from Pennsylvania though, and every fifth person in California, has or had, a real estate license. Carol had been keeping herself busy with a minor face lift and a home remodel after moving to Red Grape. John was a serious man with a mind for science, not business. He had lost his last job because budgets had been cut and because he paid no attention to office politics. No one wanted a report alarming the public about the possibility of earth quakes brought on by the new technology of fracking. A sensible man would have worded the reports differently, and with an eye toward calming the public. But John only dealt in facts. He was a geologist. Unfortunately, this lack of caution was in John's nature; his last job had taught him nothing of the world of politics and big business; the greatest part of his life had been spent doing lab and field work in Baha, Mexico. Carol had hated such third world countries. Instead, she liked her afternoon cocktails. When they moved to Red Grape, Carol and John dined out almost every night. Carol just did not cook. Despite the frequent evenings out, she and John had not been on good terms since John had lost his last job. Carol thought he was a fool and frequently told him so. John had taken up running when they moved to California, which helped him lower his blood pressure, lower his cholesterol and eliminate the stress in his life caused by his job and most of all, his wife. The protein shakes and the daily jogging had become a ritual with John. The abandoned vineyard next to their home had been a peaceful place so out of time and a great place to run in solitude. Once an active vineyard, the entire property stood untended, although the occasional grape was still present. This move to the small town of Red Grape had been hard on Carol. She was doing her best to age gracefully and her latest face lift had healed well. Harrisburg, Pennsylvania had been their home for twenty years. Yet, she and John had been forced to sell their five thousand square foot home, a traditional brick home that she had personally decorated. When John lost his job, Carol came unglued. She knew they could afford far less home in Napa, California. Worse yet, Red Grape, was a boring little berg, a town far from the coast with only one movie theatre and few amenities apart from that. Carol had been livid! Spring in Harrisburg was a cultural event, and her real estate contacts were endless there.

When Beau Geyser had approached Carol to oversee the Land Use Committee of Red Grape, she had been delighted at the change of fortune. This opportunity gave her a chance to meet developers and politically connected people in Red Grape. She had already received a huge commission from reviewing a purchase contract and for signing her name as realtor to a transaction that passed a parcel of a new developer's project over to Beau.

The mayor had been livid about John's report on water that alluded to potential contamination of the water supply and the damage to water quality caused by fracking. Over several dinners, Beau had wooed Carol into seeing things his way. Beau used, flattery, martinis, and a couple of juicy real estate commissions to get Carol to maneuver John into rewriting the report on the water contamination issue and on fracking itself. It had been her job to get John to re-write the report in a positive tone. John had flatly refused; he obviously just did not know how things worked in the world of business. It had been relatively easy for Carol to obtain a large supply of one hundred milligrams of powdered cortisol from a Canadian vendor on line, one detail of John's death that Carol left out of her conversation with the local sheriff. After all, John had been a runner, he cared about his health, he drank protein shakes every day, and he ran to reduce stress and to ensure his health.

Carol had finally given up trying to persuade John to change his report. She never really expected the cortisol to do more than slow John down; she certainly never expected him to collapse from a heart attack on a jogging trail. He had not come home from his run on a Friday afternoon, and in fact, Carol had no idea when John had left for his run. The time could have been eight am. She actually had not noticed that John was missing all day. At about four o-clock, Carol walked into their bedroom and noticed that John's keys and wallet were on his dresser, and his car was in the garage. So, at some time during the day he had gone for a run. Carol noticed that John's khaki slacks were on the chair by the bed. When did she see him last? When she woke up he was gone. She just never felt concerned about that. But, now it was time to head out for their usual early bird special. Martinis were two for one until six pm at the Chit Chat Lounge, so where in the hell was John? Carol went outside and took a cursory walk in the direction of the abandoned vineyard, used by hikers and joggers. She had passed that woman Helen who wrote the local cooking blog; she was also a runner, at about four o-clock. "Excuse me," said Carol. And Helen had stopped with a smile. "Hello!" said Helen still running in place. "Hi. Did you see an older man on the trail? I seem to have misplaced my husband," said Carol. Helen laughed, "Sorry, not today, you are Mrs. Marcel right?" "Yes!" said Carol. "We just moved here a few months ago." "I thought so. Welcome to the community," said Helen. "Thank you," said Carol. "We moved here from Harrisburg, Pennsylvania and I am still getting used to California weather. All this sunshine; don't you worry about your skin?" "You will love it," said Helen. "This is a quiet neighborhood, so safe. Nothing ever happens here; unless you count the occasional skin cancer." Helen laughed at her own little joke. Carol did not laugh. "Stock up on sun screen. Well I am off. I will send any wandering husband your way."

Helen laughed. And, Carol walked back to her home and began to worry.

At seven pm, Carol called the police and reported her husband missing. Carol had answered all of the sheriff's questions about her husband's daily routine at least four times. She and Sheriff Goodman had been over and over the facts the day of John's death. Carol had answered the same questions at least four times. It was clear that the police were not happy with the cause of death for her husband, John. Carol stood on the deck of her small refurbished home in Red Grape. The deck needed to be replaced, she noted to distract her mind form John's disappearance. She would have to contact a contractor if she wanted to get top dollar for this house. Yes, there was life insurance. Yes, they had an argument the night before and she had slept late, John being gone when she woke up. Sheriff Goodwin had waited for the autopsy report indicating heart failure. No obvious cause? Yet, why had Carol waited so long to call the police? If they had found him sooner, he may have survived. No one ever knows. The sheriff, for some reason, seemed to treat Carol as a suspect. They always look to the family first in a murder, so, that was how he was trained. But, John had heart failure, he wasn't murdered! Yes, he had been upset at work. Sheriff Goodwin wanted to know what they were fighting about the night before John died.

"The same as usual Sheriff, his work ethic; his damn work ethic!" said Carol. "Can you be more specific, Mrs. Marcel?" said Sheriff Goodwin. "John was a scientist, sheriff. His work involved risk calculations related to water, and fracking in a geothermal field, which John considered a high risk. It was very complicated. His immediate supervisor at the city did not like his report on the ground water supply. His research involved water conservation and water management for the city. John was angry about his boss's response to his report. They wanted him to change it." "They?" asked Sheriff Goodwin. "Who exactly are 'they'?" "The City of Red Grape Water Department," said Helen in exasperation. "Did your husband mention a name?" Carol went on, "Business men do not want to hear the truth. They want a report that supports their mission of growth for a community. John was bucking the system again," Carol went on. "Mrs. Marcel," Sheriff Goodwin interrupted, "did John ever mention, who did not like his report?" Helen was rewinding John's rant in her mind. "Well, Jordan Loggs did not like the report. You know Jordan Loggs, he works for some communication's firm. He says he is a media consultant. Sheriff, this is not the kind of media report the city wants. John never understood that; he was a geek. A scientist!" "Thank you, Mrs. Marcel, I will get back to you with any new developments. And, again we are so sorry for your loss." Carol went into the house and made a martini, a double!

CHAPTER SEVENTEEN

Helen Keeps Anna in the Loop

Helen called Anna the next day to tell her what had passed between her sister, Sherry, and Rusty, and to pass on the information she gathered from her husband, Brad. The questions about John Marcel and his possible heart failure on a jogging trail were astounding! Anna listened in astonishment; she knew how brutal Beau Geyser could be. Many of the homeless people in Napa feared him. Napa was a place to hire labor for odd jobs, and by hiring homeless people, there was less chance that there would be complaints about mistreatment or that employees would file law suits. The possibility of Geyser's having something to do with Carol Marcel's husband and his death was frightening to Anna. Helen reminded Anna of their emergency plan. "Remember, if Beau gets angry or alarms you, grab your cell phone and handbag and get out the door. Do not drive. Your old car is no match for a beamer. I do not trust Beau, meet me at the old stone house at St. Samuel's Vineyard. Keep a back pack with your personal stuff and be ready to run. Do not try to reason with Beau Geyser!" "Okay," said Anna, "we can do this!"

CHAPTER EIGHTEEN

She Didn't Love Him

The next morning, Carol Marcel pulled a flyer off her mail box. *Rusty Waters, Contractor, call for a free estimate.* Carol thought of the condition of the porch and called Rusty. The appointment was set for that afternoon. It was a Monday in early June and it was hot. Carol looked at the muscular man in his mid-thirties and invited him in. "So, Mr. Waters do you have references?" "Yes, I can provide them. What work do you need done? By the way, you have a lovely home." Carol sniffed as if something smelled bad. "This house is nothing compared to my last home and I intend to sell it soon. I want the front porch replaced, as it has dry rot. That is the first thing a potential buyer will see. The house must be pristine. Give me a written quote, and estimate of your hours and time to complete." "Okay," said Rusty. "This is such a lovely neighborhood, I am surprised you want to move." "This is a small town with no culture. I will probably move back to Harrisburg." "You and your husband?" asked Rusty. "No, my husband recently passed away." "Oh, I am so sorry, I didn't know, you seem so young; how did he die?" Carol was flattered and she answered, "My husband was a runner, Mr. Waters, and he over did it jogging on a trail. He never listened to me about such things." "Well, okay," said Rusty, "let me take a look around and I will write up a quote for the work to be done." Rusty went out on the porch, took some measurements and left a quote for Carol. When she took the quote, she had a martini in her hand. "If this is estimate is okay with you, let me know your time frame for the work to be done," said Rusty. Carol responded, "I will give you a call, Mr. Waters. Thank you for stopping by." Task complete, Rusty got in his truck and drove home. Carol Marcel was not mourning the loss of her husband.

CHAPTER NINETEEN

Andy Goodman
Get Ready

The Sheriff's station was in an older building off a cross street in downtown Red Grape. There was plenty of parking in front of the creamy adobe colored building which sat back from the street. The arched windows in front of the Sheriff's offices faced the street and the Sheriff could look out on the street and the quiet town; too perfect. Sheriff Goodman took a deep breath and sipped his cold coffee. He was at his cluttered desk when Cindy, a trainee, put another autopsy report on his desk. Andy Goodman was a thorough man. He had been a small town sheriff for ten years after having been burned out on working the mean streets of San Francisco for too many years. The chances of becoming a victim of a violent crime in San Francisco had been 1 in 140. Andy's personal opinion was that the convenience of the Bay Area Rapid Transit system, BART, criminals using cell phones to warn one another, and the lure of burglarizing expensive real estate had combined to become a recipe for crime in San Francisco. Criminals knew there was money in the toney neighborhoods of San Francisco. Any woman carrying a Coach handbag and commuting on BART was a target. The criminals either followed the potential victim home and planned the B & E for another day, or just grabbed her handbag to be sold on the underground market or on eBay. Criminals were becoming ever more organized, and the police had little chance of catching these low lifes, once they jumped on BART. Andy had seen too many women maimed or killed over their expensive handbags. It had been time to get out of the city. Andy had decided to transfer to this small town just ten miles outside of Napa. Red Grape was his town and thankfully very little happened there. There may be a rowdy drunk or the occasional domestic dispute and that was it. In ten years, there had not been a single murder in town. He did not like people dying under any condition in Red Grape, and Andy had a cop's sense of unease about the way John Marcel had died; alone on a hiking trail. His body had not been found for over eight hours; His wife had either not noticed him missing or chose not to care. People are funny. But, he didn't think that Carol was a murderer, just another married couple whose marriage had drifted apart perhaps. Andy left the door open on Carol as a suspect for now. After questioning Carol four times Andy finally got another suspect for a possible murder. Maybe he was wrong, but better to probe a bit than let this just slide under the rug. John Marcel had enemies. Andy did not like Mayor Geyser or Jordan Loggs. Why did this small town need a lobbyist? Geyser had moved to Red Grape from Napa about ten years ago, and suddenly got real interested in both local politics and in real estate. The city council used to consist of community volunteers. Now, a seat on the city council belonged to professional politicians with money and connections. Andy had requested further toxicology testing and a copy of the water report John Marcel had been working on. Settling down to read the report, Andy found what he was looking for; cortisol and adrenaline are common metabolites in a victim of heart failure. But, this autopsy showed very high levels of cortisol, as if John had been taking steroids of cortisol. He was a fifty five year old geologist specializing in water conservation, not a body builder. Andy decided to check in at the city offices and search the desk of John Marcel. There should be computer files, correspondence, and emails, and that water report that Carol Marcel spoke of should also be available. That should be hot reading this evening. He would not necessarily understand a water report, but he could focus on it as his wife watched her reality episodes on television. "Bernie, I am going over to city hall; keep an eye on things will you?" Bernie, his deputy, fairly sprinted over to take up the boss's chair. Bernie loved playing chief when Andy was investigating or monitoring the town. Nothing much happened here, not like Napa where there was loads of crime, and you might actually get the chance to do a dirty Harry thing one day. Dirty Harry was Bernie's idol! He drew his gun, and swiveled in the chair, "Go ahead make my day," Bernie said. Cindy, the dispatcher, laughed her head off. "Bernie you are going to kill someone one of these days with that gun," she chortled.

This comment however, did not rattle Bernie; he would have been glad to have the chance to apprehend a real criminal one day.

Cindy turned back to her monitor and continued typing. Bernie was a kick to be around. She loved working for the sheriff's office. Cindy had been glad to get out of the city council offices. Too much tension over there; politics had become a blood sport on the town council, with shouting, name calling and choosing up sides on issues. She was glad to be out of there.

"Are you feeling lucky punk? Well are you?" Bernie went on. "That comment," said Cindy, "will be remembered. Don't you have work to do?"

"Pardon me for interrupting," said Rusty standing at the counter with a broad smile on his face and a cowboy hat in his hand, "but if he is really feeling dangerous, maybe he can help me." Bernie spun around in Sheriff's Goodwin's chair and put on his serious look. He asked, "How can we help you?"

"Sheriff, I need some help on a possible crime regarding injury and coercion of a young woman who lives in Red Grape, and she may have been injured by one of your local residents. Who could help me?"

"Yes sir, well the woman would have to file a complaint," said Bernie, "And what if she has been threatened about coming to the police about the matter?" asked Rusty. "The office of the prosecutor is charged with the responsibility for prosecutions in its jurisdiction. Anyone can request help from the Napa Special Investigations Bureau," said Bernie.

Brad smiled and asked for the address of the Napa Special Investigations Bureau. With that Rusty reached to shake Bernie's hand and thanked him. "You have been very helpful. Nice to know Red Grape employs such knowledgeable law enforcement staff." "No problem," Bernie responded. Cindy watched the tall stranger with the muscular arms walk to his truck. "You could have at least gotten his name," said Cindy when Rusty was out of hearing range. "He better come in here again or you are dead meat, Dirty Bernie," said Cindy.

CHAPTER TWENTY

Who Can We Trust?

A week later, the residents of Red Grape opened a new issue of *The Grape Leaf*. Kate had been working for a week on her editorial. The headlines read, *Who Can We Trust?* Although it was a dangerous gambit, Kate had decided to use her most recent research on Mayor Geyser; his affairs. Not only had Kate talked with Barb Geyser, she had met Sally, the bar tender, a woman who was privy to the comings and goings of many locals in Red Grape. And a bar was always a good place to get information. Was there ever a time when a drunk man was shy after three gin and tonics? And how they loved to talk about their self-importance and their latest big score, whether personal or professional. Beau Geyser was no different. After a couple of gin martinis, Beau was very open about his accomplishments in Red Grape. Beau was well known for draping his arm over the young servers and copping a feel. Sally was well aware of Beau's habits and female friends. Kate had always liked Sally; a tell it like it is kind of woman.

Sally's education came from the infamous school of hard knocks. Kate had lunch with Sally at La Bou Bakery on a sunny Monday. La Bou served fresh baked breads and a choice of two different frittatas every day. Sally ordered the spinach and cheese frittata with warm rye bread. Kate ordered the Ortega chili and cheese frittata and they both had mint ice tea. While they waited for their lunch, Kate asked Sally about gossip at the Chit Chat. "Oh, you know, Kate, same old stuff, just new faces. None of the servers will wait on Beau since he loves to grope them, so I always have to serve him. Now he has a new young girl friend," said Sally. "I heard," said Kate. "Do they come in often?" "He usually has his little babe meet him in a corner booth midweek in the back of the bar. I don't know who he thinks he's fooling, with his civic minded "big shot" of our town? The guy is a sleazy lecherous old man who likes to slobber on young woman. The servers refuse to serve him. He is abusive, too. I have seen his explosions." "His philandering is going to get him in trouble one of these days. A couple of weeks ago, a young woman came in late, ordered wine and waited for Beau to come in. He must have been late because she was ticked off when he finally showed up. I think it was a Thursday night after the city council meeting." Their food arrived and Sally went on. "Anyway, they got into a hot argument. There was a new guy in town at the bar, good lookin', too. He seemed a bit interested when Beau and the young gal got hot. Beau lunged at the girl and grabbed her wrist. Glasses flew spilled wine all over, and the romantic evening was done. Personally, I think that guy, Rusty was his name, was about to deck him. The girl was yelling about developer bribes and land deals." Kate was finishing her frittata. "You lead an exciting life Sally." "Yep, I am going to write a book one day" "You should you know," said Kate. The women finished their lunches and Kate said, "I couldn't interest you in adopting a kitten could I?" "Not yet, Kate, my landlord said no pets. One day I will have my own home, then I will get a cat." "You know where to come," said Kate. They both laughed and parted just outside La Bou.

When Kate got home, she had a message from her neighbor, Helen, who left a message about her sister adopting a kitten. Well of course, thought Kate. The kitten that sweet young girl Anna had dropped off was a perfect match for Helen's sister, Sherry. They made plans to meet the following day. Kate prepared tuna sandwiches and ice tea, and, over lunch, asked Helen what she thought of the water rate issue going on in Red Grape. "Well, my husband's comment was that Beau Geyser is a crook." "That is certainly true, but so many people in our community just go along with his decisions anyway. I was glad to see your husband at the last city council meeting, by the way." "Yes," agreed Helen. "Brad was not happy to hear the council approve another developer's request to rezone and build more homes on the Saint Samuel Vineyard property," said Helen. "He is a piece of work, I have known his wife for years and she has given up trying to change the bastard," said Kate. Helen and Sherry looked at each other. "So, Kate, I have run across some information that would be very damning to Beau Geyser and his position as mayor. But I am not sure who to talk to. I thought you might know how to leak this information to the press?" Helen tilted her head in her manner of making a question without words. Kate looked surprised. "Me, no dear I do not get involved in our local paper." Sipping her iced tea, Kate looked at Helen with intelligent blue eyes. "Too risky, me with all these kitties; I stay under the radar where Beau Geyer and our city council are concerned. Beau has been known to send inspectors out and issue code violations to people who complain about his way of doing things." Kate sipped her iced tea and petted the huge tabby who had come looking for a treat. Kate pinched off a piece of her tuna sandwich for Bully, her cat. "Actually, I do know someone who writes under a pen name for the *Grape Leaf.* "Can you tell me what you have unearthed on Beau?" "Well," said Helen, "you would have to keep me out of this. Like you, I avoid the city council for my own reasons." Kate was intrigued, more secrets. Helen filled their ice tea glasses and settled in to listen to the latest Beau Geyser story.

So, Helen filled Kate in on Beau Geyser, his real estate acquisitions, the sweet young girl she met at the medical clinic and his connection to Carol Marcel. "He keeps her in his condo?" yelled Kate. "That's right," said Helen. "The young girl, Anna is her name, was in trouble in Napa, and he offered to give her a place to live, by saying it was a vacant condo he owned. Turns out, Beau expected sexual favors, in exchange for a … for a condo," said Helen. "That bastard," said Kate. Bully's hair stood up. The cat's agitation over Kate's distress was uncanny. "And, that's not all," said Helen. "The girl is terrified of him. I have seen her injuries, up close. We need to find her another place to live. She is a widow; her young husband died in the Mediterranean while deployed in the Navy." "Oh my…. I think I met her. She dropped a cat off a few months ago," said Kate. "Yes, she mentioned that, well, maybe we can find a place where she can have a cat again someday. Right now she needs to get a job and she needs to finish high school," said Helen. Then, Sherry finally spoke up, "Listen ladies, this guy is dangerous, stirring the pot is going to get hot and spicy for Beau Geyser and maybe for us, too. I do not trust him. That young girl is in danger along with anyone else who might damage his sterling reputation." Kate continued, "She's right. We need to talk to Sheriff Goodwin, before another person ends up dead on a hiking trail." Bully jumped up on the chair next to Kate. It seemed as if Bully was part of the group. He was there to protect Kate. Kate smiled. "Sometimes he thinks he is a lion. I swear he knows what we are talking about. "

"Believe me, Helen, your secrets are safe with me; we need to watch out for each other. You have opened my eyes to more secrets in Red Grape; let me assure you, that I will keep the source of this new information private. You can rely on me to be discreet." Kate paused for a minute, then said. "It's hard to believe that one man has caused so much chaos in our quiet little town. Since Beau moved here ten years ago, water rates have soared. The oil companies started fracking in the geo thermal basin, and several wineries have gone under due to wells drying up. No water means no harvest. St. Samuels went under due to the draught. Their well went dry and they could no longer afford to irrigate their ten acres of vineyards with city water. So sad really, Sam and his wife were old friends of mine and they made a great wine too. Sam was voted most likely to succeed in business in our senior class at Napa, class of '65." Helen and Sherry looked at each other and smiled, then stepped off Kate's pretty porch, and Kate walked them out to the curb. Bully kept pace with Kate. The big cat moved like a lion on prowl. He rarely left her side. "I guess this means you did not stop by to adopt a cat?" asked Kate with a sly smile. Helen turned and put her finger to her mouth to imply this was indeed a secret.

CHAPTER TWENTY-ONE

Heard it Through the Grape Vine

Sheriff Goodwin was directed to John Marcel's office by an overworked clerk named Maria Monroe, who always appeared nervous and stressed. Little wonder as she was a single mom and worked in the stressful city offices. "This office was set up for Mr. Marcel when he was hired early last year. It was a shock to all of us when he died, Sheriff. He seemed so interested in his health," said Maria. Sheriff Goodwin turned to see Maria sip her big gulp. "Did you know John very well?" he asked. "We chatted on breaks and lunch hours. He always commented on my choice of drinks. He was a health nut and did not approve of my big gulps." "Was he a coffee drinker?" asked Sheriff Goodwin. "Not that I noticed; he was really into his power drinks, and those health smoothies. You know the type, a real environmentalist, but a nice guy," concluded Maria. Sheriff Goodwin walked on to John Marcel's office. Things looked neat and clean. There was no computer on the desk. Odd, you would expect to see a computer on a geek's desk. Sheriff Goodwin started to search the desk drawers and oddly he found a flash drive in a drawer filled with personal items. A flash drive probably meant that there had been a computer on the desk at some point. The sheriff also found some prescription bottles including Atenolol 100 mg. (blood pressure), baby aspirin, centrum vitamins, and a container of protein powder, along with a package of plastic spoons. John Marcel was obviously a man concerned with good health. He took vitamins, watched his blood pressure, jogged and drank protein shakes. Something was wrong with such a man getting a fatal heart attack. Andy next looked at the file cabinet, which was unlocked. He opened the top drawer to find an assortment of files filled with correspondence and reports. One fat file folder was labeled Fracking Dangers, consisting mostly of periodicals, nothing generated by John Marcel. A large bound report from the Endocrine Society and California Department of Conservation (DOC) contained a public notice of the proposed regulations for the use of well stimulation in oil and gas production. Yep, ponderous reading, thought Andy.

He admonished himself for not searching this office the night John Marcel's body was found. Lots of people had access to Marcel's office in the last month. Andy filled an evidence bag with the medications, the flash drive and, as an afterthought, he grabbed the protein powder and the large file marked Fracking Dangers.

On his way out, Andy stopped at Maria's desk again. Maria had tears running down her face. "Are you okay Maria?" asked Andy in his fatherly voice. "Sure, this is just a stressful place to work." The sheriff had not heard the conversation Maria had on the phone while Andy had been searching John Marcel's office. Maria answered a phone call from Beau Geyser and mentioned that the sheriff had stopped to ask some questions and was in John Marcel's office. Beau had screamed at Maria, "You dummy!" Maria knew her job was on the line and she needed this job; she had children to feed and rent to pay. She had been instructed to clean up John Marcel's office. She did not know that she was supposed to have removed John's personal things, along with John's computer. "You are one dumb blond, Maria. You better have that computer in a safe place, and no record of that report on fracking, are we clear on that?" "Yes, Mr. Geyser. I removed John's report from the file, just like you told me to do." Maria hated to be called dumb. She just did her job, and did not know why John's report on fracking was so important to the mayor. Regardless, she did not like removing things from John's office. Maria had been friendly with John, and besides, she felt that his wife would want John's personal things, so she had left them in his desk drawer. John Marcel's computer was in the broom closet under a pile of cleaning supplies, per her instructions. Taking a computer from the building seemed wrong, and so she had merely moved it.

This information, however, bothered Sheriff Goodwin; he

would have liked to question Maria a bit further but, she looked wrung out today. Sheriff Goodwin decided to drop John's medications at the police lab for analysis and to see what was on the flash drive belonging to John Marcel. Yet, just as he was leaving city hall, Andy turned to ask Maria a quick question.

"Maria, did you straighten up Mr. Marcel's office after he passed away?" he asked. "I wondered, because things looked so neat in there." "Yes, Sheriff, I was asked to straighten things up," answered Maria. "Good, I thought so. I will speak to Mr. Geyser and get his statement on John Marcel later. You do a great job for those bozos, Maria, I hope they appreciate you. I know you are leaving for night school in a few minutes, but we still need to talk about John Marcel. When is a good time for you?" Maria looked up and said, "Maybe tomorrow, sheriff, and can we keep my name out of this?" Andy asked, "What do you mean?" Maria answered, "Well, just do not mention to Beau that you intend to speak to me; he is already angry that I did not clean out all of John's office.... I need this job sheriff." Andy took this in; just as he suspected, Beau Geyser was pressuring Maria to withhold information. Andy responded, "I can come to your home and we can have a private chat, how would that be?" Maria took a deep breath and nodded. "Sheriff...you should know that John and I were pretty good friends. He helped me with homework, especially on geology and on some of my papers. He was a very nice man, and I will miss him." The sheriff said, "About nine tonight, is that okay?" Maria nodded. Andy was out the door. Maria didn't know why, but she felt better.

CHAPTER TWENTY-TWO

A Change Is in the Air

Maria Monroe had been working at the city offices and attending night school for several years. She had two kids in middle school and an ex-husband who refused to contribute to their kids' support. Maria carried the load. She made sure her kids did their homework. She wanted a better life for her kids. John Marcel had encouraged her to change her major to water conservation management. John had been the one bright spot in Maria's day, working for the city government. Beau Geyser was an ego maniac, a real control freak who thought he could negotiate anything. Maria felt sorry for his wife, Barbara. John's wife was a cool one and she wondered why she often called to speak to Beau Geyser instead of to her husband. Something to do with real estate and money was her guess. One afternoon, she had seen Carol and Beau having a quiet lunch at Perino's, an upscale bistro in town. They had been deep in conversation. Oh well, stupid woman, thought Maria. Wait till he turns on her she thought, and he would. Maria had shared many lunch hours with John Marcel, and listened to his theory on fracking, the dangers of groundwater contamination, and on the continuing water shortage in California, and especially the Napa Valley and their town. John had shown her the web site created by the Endocrine Society and the new research linking fracking and ground water contamination, and studies linking low sperm count to fracking contamination of drinking water. Maria was amazed to find out that a study done in 2013 linked low birth rates to areas supplying tainted ground water to Red Grape, due to the fracking chemicals and EDC's also known as endocrine-disrupting chemical pollution. The levels of EDC's were way too high in the Red Grape water supply and John had written a report that explained the dangers to the population of the town. Eventually, the contaminated water found its way into the city ground water supply. John's report was not well received by the city water department. He had been asked to rewrite the report. John was angry and frustrated. She and John usually ate in the lunch room. Maria had run out for his fruit smoothies and her big gulp. At their lunches together, John stirred his protein powder into his cup and coached Maria with her homework. He had helped her with a geology report that required the documentation of a geological eco system. John continued to rant over a State water contamination report and another document from the Endocrine Society released in 2013. John had explained how things worked in terms she could understand. Removing water from a ground water source left a hole which had to be filled with new rain water that filtered down into the receiving water.

In periods of long drought, it was dangerous to remove too much ground water without replacing it in the aquifer. Earth quakes could occur when a void or empty space grew too large to support the ground above it. The practice of fracking could also trigger a quake. Water and chemicals shot into local oil wells under pressure dissolved the shale and stimulated oil and gas production, but, it was a trade-off. The oil companies got higher production, but water volume suffered and the chemicals migrated into the city's water supply. Maria had not destroyed all of John's work. In fact, she had mailed a draft of John's report to *The Grape Leaf,* the day before the sheriff had come in to search John's office. It had been over a month since his death. The town needed to know the truth about the water supply. If Beau found out, she would lose her job. Politicians never lost their jobs, they just called in their favors and got re-elected. Beau even had his very own lobbyist, Jordan Loggs, to handle the media and do damage control by lying to the community. The Red Grape city council was a well-oiled machine fully funded by their sugar daddy oil companies and land developers.

CHAPTER TWENTY-THREE

Gridlock Traffic

It had been a hell of a drive home for Brad during an unusually hot, dry spell in June, turning the freeway pavement hot and the drivers irritable. The traffic was bumper to bumper thru town and the mystery train held up commuters for fifteen minutes. No one seemed to be able to fix this quirk in the phantom train. The bells rang and the guard rails came down. Drivers sat in the oppressive heat and no train passed through the main street out of town. Brad arrived home wilted. In the drive way was the current issue of *The Grape Leaf*. It felt dry enough to ignite. Brad carried the paper in through the garage. Helen had been on her cell phone and said, "Talk later," as Brad came through the door. The smell of tomatoes lifted Brad's mood. Helen had made his favorite pasta with fresh tomatoes and garlic that smelled like summer in Tuscany simmering on the stove. A bottle of crisp rose from St. Samuels Vineyard was cooling in the fridge. Since St. Samuels had stopped producing, bottles of their famous rose had become highly collectible. Brad put his jacket, tie and the paper on a chair in the kitchen, and asked, "How was your day?" "Good," said Helen, "hot, but good. I tried to go for a run, but the heat was too much, I didn't get far. I don't remember it being this hot in May, ever." Helen opened the special bottle of rose, and poured them each a glass. "What's the occasion?" Brad asked, as he opened the local paper and read the large headlines. Helen paused and gazed out the kitchen window at the dry hillsides. "Oh, I was thinking of St. Samuels today; I miss their place in the community....and their wine." "Now what?" asked Brad, *Who can we trust?* Was printed in bold type across the local *Grape Leaf* paper, by Stormy Day.

Brad was sitting with Helen after dinner, reflecting on what he had read in the latest issue of, *The Grape Leaf*. The author was still using a pen name, and for good reason. He or she was making the Red Grape city council look corrupt. The headlines of *The Grape Leaf* read.

Who can we trust?
By Stormy Day

Some Americans are wondering why some cities in California are ignoring the drought while other cities in California are trucking in water. Development after development is approved and re-zoned, when a developer buys up agricultural land with the intent to build high density housing. They need a rezone permit from our city council, and, they always get it!

A little research will show you who owns investment properties here in Red Grape. How many rentals are owned by elected members of the city council?

Who benefits from these new developments? The contractors, realtors, investors, oil companies, developers and landscapers all benefit from these large, incredibly profitable, projects.

These new homes appeal to families who want to get out of the big city. Who can blame them? But, most home owners do not know what is happening to our ground water. A look at recent water bills will tell you that the water rates increase every year. Now we are advised to use less water! Who votes for these rate increases? And, who is monitoring the quality of our water? The Red Grape City Council.

The city of Red Grape hired an expert, about a year ago, to evaluate our ground water supply and quality, and proposed increased production of ground water wells. The expert prepared his initial findings, which were never released to the public. A copy of John Marcel's report was mailed to the offices of the Grape Leaf, addressed to the editor three weeks after John passed away. Sadly, John Marcel cannot be queried about this report. The practice of fracking was mentioned in Mr. Marcel's preliminary report; a report yet to be released to the public; the draft was under review by our town media specialist and county council. The draft contained warnings of hydraulic fracturing in rural areas like Red Grape and the risk of water contamination, specifically EDC's or, endocrine-disrupting chemical pollution and earth quakes. Without safeguards, fracking could lead to unsafe water quality and subsiding landscapes. Fracking also uses water needed to supply residents and to irrigate vineyards. Each and every well requires millions of gallons of water during the fracking process. In arid places like California, this could mean less water for irrigation and rural communities. Red Grape suffers from over development and a shortage of safe ground water for residents and for our vineyards. Yet, our city council continues to approve new developments. Why?

Vineyard after vineyard has gone under in the last few years due to the drought, the cost of water and poor city management. Should we trust our city council? Who are our city leaders? When did our city council members become real estate investors?

Spend an hour at the Cut n' Curl and catch up on the latest "love gone wrong" in town. Who has a wife and a girlfriend in Red Grape? Stop in for a glass of local rose' at the Chit Chat Inn and catch the latest lovers tiffs.

"Things are hot here, but I expect they are hotter down at the town council building," said Brad. "I wouldn't want to be Beau Geyser about now. Stormy Day, whoever she is, if she is a she, is giving the locals some hot gossip in today's local paper. If I were the sheriff, I would be wondering who provided that water report to the local paper." Helen smiled and sipped her wine. "Brad, do you think it is possible that our little neighbor, Kate, the animal lover, could be writing these editorials?" Silence from Brad. "Do you?" pushed Helen. Brad looked away from the news and looked at Helen, who had that tilt to her head that was a physical question mark. Brad looked at the paper again. "Kate is a smart old gal. I saw her at the city council meeting; she is well informed and seems to know everyone down there. What is really alarming is that water report. Who leaked it to the local paper? It had to come from John Marcel. Yet, John died over a month ago of a heart attack. So, who had access to John's report? Was it his wife, or a city employee, or is it just a red herring used to make the mayor look bad? You can bet our sheriff is going to be asking some tough questions." Just then, Helen's cell phone rang. "Hi!" said Helen "What? Calm down!" Brad looked at Helen, who was becoming animated. "Anna, slow down, where are you? Okay, okay, okay, I will come and get you. Do not drive your car! Let him think you are still there. Stay off the road. Yes, I will pick you up at the abandoned vineyard, fifteen minutes!" Brad looked at his blond wife, the all American girl. "What is up Helen?"

CHAPTER TWENTY-FOUR

I'll Be There

"You have to come with me Brad, I have rescued another stray and she needs my help." "Who is Anna, Helen?" asked Brad. Helen had her car keys and was heading out through the garage. "Bring your cell phone and a flash light," she said. Brad had no idea what his wife was up to, but he was not letting her leave without him. In the car, Helen told Brad about her initial meeting with Anna at the medical clinic. The girl was terrified of Beau Geyser, and with good reason. The phone call was from Anna. Beau had called her and was in a roaring rage, she repeated, apparently after reading the latest editorial; he wanted her out of his condo and was on his way over to physically evict her. "She has no lease Brad. That is how Beau Geyser has been manipulating her He means to tell the sheriff that Anna is trespassing if she calls him for help. That is why Beau would not allow her to get a job or make friends in town," Helen explained hurriedly. "How did you meet her?" asked Brad. "The doctor's office when I went in about the hiccups. Let's go." Beau told her to pack and he was going to drive her back to Napa tonight. She knew she would not have time to pack, so she called me. I told her to grab her back pack and load it with her personal things, in case she needs to run. Well, she needs to run, and fast. Our arranged meeting place is the old stone house at the abandoned vineyard. "Tonight, Beau was in a rage," Anna said. Brad drove to the old vineyard behind the new condo development. "Yes, I told her to leave her car so that Beau would think she was still in the condo. That would give her more time," said Helen. "Good thinking Helen, Beau does not know about you, I take it?" "No, that is our advantage." He did not count on her making a friend," Helen said smugly. "Why not just call the sheriff, Helen?" "Anna does not have a lease with Brad. He will have the law on his side. Legally, she is trespassing, and Beau Geyser would tell the sheriff that she has no formal lease and that she has been squatting on his property. Brad, we have to hide Anna and get her to a shelter. Beau Geyser stands to be exposed by a young woman who he has been keeping in his condo in exchange for sexual favors. His sterling reputation is about to get tarnished."

Brad and Helen drove thru the town's dark country roads. They passed vineyard after vineyard; rows of grape vines stood guard like rows of soldiers. Some were producing, but many vineyards had folded due to the drought in California. The dry vines were a reminder of just how precious water is to all agriculture. California needed water badly. Water, the precious life giving fluid, was running out; wells had run dry, and city water was becoming less affordable by the month. Brad and Helen passed the new developments and abandoned vineyards until they came to a wooden arch above a driveway with the words, St. Samuels Vineyard. "That bastard... there, turn there Brad!" And Helen pointed to the delivery entrance off the main road, and directly onto the dirt road through St. Samuels Vineyard. Brad got out of the car to check an old wooden gate, and as Brad opened it, a hinge broke, and he had to drag the gate to admit Helen's car onto the property. Helen pulled in and Brad closed the gate behind her. Just then, they noticed lights approaching them down the two lane highway from town. Helen quickly turned off her car lights. The dirt road was rutted and twisted. Dry grape vines eerily stood watch as if they were arthritic patriots unwilling to give up their posts. The driveway consisted of a large curve. Helen grabbed the flash light to keep them on the old dirt road which had for years been used by trucks and vineyard workers. She did not want to be spotted from the condos adjacent to the old vineyard. Brad and Helen pulled up in front of the old stone house which had been so charming at one time. Helen saw no one. "I am worried Brad, what if they took her?" Brad had been mentally putting the pieces of this puzzle together. His wife had somehow stumbled into someone's scheme to manipulate development in Red Grape. It was all about money, land and water. The young girl they intended to help knew too much and stood to shatter the reputation of the honorable mayor. And suppose John Marcel did not have a heart attack; what if he had been poisoned somehow? Helen called Anna's cell and, it rang and rang before going to voice mail. Suddenly, Brad realized that they should have called the sheriff, but there was no time now. They had to find that girl, stash her, and then contact the police. At that moment, a small girl, who looked more teen ager than woman, rounded the old stone house. Anna had on jeans, a dark, long sleeved shirt, and a back pack. The only thing visible was her light blond hair illuminated by the full moon. Helen got out of the car and said, "thank God, we thought he grabbed you!" Anna, held a finger to her lips. "They are searching for me. I saw flash lights in the rows of vines. Beau kept calling on my cell so, I turned it off." Brad saw a light sweeping searchingly along the rows of twisted vines about five hundred feet from the main house. Beau had evidently gone to the condo and was now searching on foot for Anna. Brad waved them into the car and took over the wheel. Brad, Helen and Anna drove in total darkness back towards the main road. Brad kept his speed low, and did not use his break lights, something he had learned as a teenager. The curve in the driveway blocked the sight of their car. As they approaching the broken gate, Brad jumped out to lift it aside enough for the car to move onto the main road. "Helen, call 911 and, get Sheriff Goodwin on the line," shouted Brad.

CHAPTER TWENTY-FIVE

Something Is Blowing in the Wind

Bernie, the deputy, had the night shift and was sitting in Sheriff Goodwin's big chair reading the local *Grape Leaf* at about nine pm that early June evening . As usual, his iPod was plugged into the station sound system. On these slow night shifts, Bernie loved to listen to his own selection of tunes. The sound track from *The Good, the Bad and The Ugly* played as he sipped weak coffee with powdered creamer. It seemed as if the heat had sapped the town's energy and not much was going on, so he was startled by the 911 call coming in. "911, what's your emergency?" asked Bernie, hoping for some action. "We need help; where is Sheriff Goodwin?" demanded Helen. "This is Helen Elson; I am in a car with my husband and with Anna McKinney. I think we are being followed." Bernie asked her, "Why do you think you are in danger?" Helen took an exasperated breath. "Bernie, get the Sheriff!" "Now calm down, Helen. Are you near your home?" responded Bernie. "No, we are out near St. Samuels Vineyard. I got a call from a friend of mine who has been threatened by Beau Geyser. She hid and we, my husband and I, picked her up. Someone was stalking her in the vineyard, Bernie. Move it. Okay?" said Helen. "Okay, calm down," said Bernie. "She called me for help out near Beau Vista Condos," responded Helen, the exasperation climbing in her voice. "Hold on Helen, what is your location?" asked Bernie as he began to write. "We are in my car and driving towards town on Pino Road, and it looks like a silver car is coming fast and gaining on us!" She nearly screamed. "Sheriff Goodwin is off duty tonight, Helen" "Well, call him Bernie. This is urgent!" Just then, the silent alarm went off at the Grape Leaf Publishing Office on Vino Road. And then, a second 911 call came in: it blinked as Bernie called for Cindy, the dispatcher. The caller ID indicated that the caller was Kate Summers. "Cindy get in here, I need help now!" Bernie bellowed. Cindy had been in the break room reading an adventure novel. "What now Bernie?" yelled Cindy, annoyed at being interrupted. "Call Napa, we need back up, and pick up that 911 caller," ordered Bernie. "Hello, 911 what is your emergency?" queried Cindy. This was her first time on the 911 line. "This is Kate Summers, send help I have an intruder!"

Cindy knew the routine. Dispatch a car and keep the caller on the phone. "A Napa patrol is on the way, Kate. Where is the intruder now?" Bernie said, "Hold on, Helen, there is a break in on your street; drive directly to the Sheriff's station." Bernie then called Sheriff Goodwin, who was just getting home. "All Hell is breaking loose, sheriff; we need you. Two 911 calls: a break in and a possible attempted kidnap." Within minutes, police vehicles were converging on Red Grape from Napa, where the responding officers were having coffee at the Model Bakery on First Street in Napa. "Damn, nothing ever happens in Red Grape. Did I hear that right? Two 911 calls and a B & E?" Officer Stone shook his head and drove. "We better call for more units." "Helen, Bernie here, drive straight in to the station. Do not go home; there is trouble on your street. I have just dispatched a patrol car to Kate Summer's home." "Intruder!" called Cindy. "And, Sheriff Goodwin is on his way." The patrol cars had their sirens going as they pulled up in front of Kate Summer's home. Two officers responded, and boxed in the house, both back and front. The cats were making a hell of a racket in her garage. One officer knocked on the front door, but Kate was still on the phone with Cindy. Someone had been in her bedroom, a tall man. Her cat Bully had leaped at the man and possibly scratched him. Kate heard him scream. "His scream alerted me. I woke up and a tall man was standing over me. Bully jumped on his head. He screamed and ran. I dialed 911. I am not sure if he is still in the house." Kate said to Cindy. "Kate, an officer is coming in your back door now. Is it open?" "I'm not sure," responded Kate. "Kate wait! Wait until the officers get to you," advised Cindy continuing to calm Kate. "They are downstairs now," said Kate. The officers cleared the downstairs rooms and made their way upstairs to Kate's bedroom. As they kicked open the door with guns drawn, the biggest cat they had ever seen growled like a lion. Kate grabbed Bully before he could attack the police officers. "Good kitty," said Kate.

CHAPTER TWENTY-SIX

Don't Go Out Tonight

By the time Sheriff Goodwin got to his office, the town was exploding with a forced entry, various burglaries, police cars in pursuit, and a possible attempted kidnapping. Napa had responded to the town's crime wave with back up. "Where is the couple who were being pursued?" asked Andy. Bernie said, "I put them in the break room; they are rattled." When Andy went into the break room, Anna was crying, and Helen was comforting her. Brad was talking about being chased by a silver beamer. All three were sure it was Beau Geyser. As Brad and Helen told their story of Anna calling for help, the Sheriff noticed the *Grape Leaf* open on his desk. This was no coincidence. The expose' was to come out in the paper today. Mayor Geyser's little girl friend got threatened, chased and rescued by Helen, a local cooking blogger. The local newspaper office was broken into, and personnel files were stolen according to a responding officer from Napa, who had briefed Andy on his way into the station. The officer took pictures and gathered the security tapes from the newspaper's CCTV. Who would want personnel files? Someone who wants the name and address of a writer who uses a pen name, thought Andy.

Sheriff Goodwin had taken the statement of Maria Monroe earlier in the evening and the lab reports showed exceptionally high levels of cortisol in John Marcel's blood. Carol had ordered Cortisol from a Canadian on line pharmacy. Things were coming together. "Put out an APB for Carol Marcel, Bernie," said Andy as he proceeded to the break room to take the statements of parties involved in the aborted kidnapping. The publisher of the local paper had also shown up with his camera. He was hoping for a good story. It was going to be a long night.

CHAPTER TWENTY-SEVEN

Earlier That Evening

At five pm, Carol Marcel was dressed and ready to head to the Chit Chat Inn for appetizers and the two for one, martinis. She was joined by Mr. McReady, who was handling John's will and other issues related to the estate. Carol Marcel met with Mr. McReady early. He was happy to help her handle her life insurance claim for her deceased husband. McReady said, "You need to provide me with the death certificate; then I can handle the life insurance and name changes on your properties, Carol. Looks like John left everything to you." At eight thirty, McReady received a call on his cell. Quickly he said, "Sorry Carol, gotta run; the wife is expecting me." McReady's wife was not the caller. Beau Geyser called and gave him a name and address. "Finish the job, and no screw ups." McReady appeared a bit shaken as he got up to leave the Chit Chat. Carol was still sipping her third martini. One of several, she had called Beau Geyser four times after reading the local *Grape Leaf.* She sat in a cozy booth and pondered her options now that her husband was dead. The life insurance money would allow her to get out of Red Grape. Yet, she did not like the fact that her husband's water report had made it into the local paper. Beau was bound to be angry. Well, no one can say she didn't do her part. In fact, she hoped that no one knew what part she had played to assure that the water report went away. She really never expected to be a party to murder, though. Beau had convinced her that better things were yet to come. But where was Beau now? At nine thirty, Carol was still waiting for Beau Geyser. Carol looked up at the sound of police sirens; two cars from Napa were responding to crime in Red Grape.

CHAPTER TWENTY-EIGHT

Can't Buy Respect

At ten o clock McReady was finally home and in a state of panic. His pants were torn, he was huffing, he had on one shoe, and he had a wet paper towel on his face. His wife had just gone to bed and was sitting with a Nora Roberts book. "What in the hell happened to you?" asked Mary. "I fell getting out of my car," said McReady. Mary threw the covers back and walked into the bathroom where her normally calm husband was dousing his reddened face with cold water. When he stood up, he had bright red claw marks on his cheeks and head. "That is not from a fall," Mary said sternly. "Well, it could have been the rose bushes." "Mitch, we do not have roses. Where were you? Your pants are torn, and where is your other shoe?" Mitch....just stood there with a big dumb look on his face, and he was trembling. His hands were braced on the basin as he looked into the mirror over the bathroom sink. "Honey," he said slowly, "I think we need to go out of town for a couple of days." "What?" Mary blurted, "The city council meets tomorrow evening; you can't just leave." Mitch walked into the bedroom and sat down facing his wife. "Mary, I think it may have been a mistake to move to Red Grape and especially to trust Beau Geyser." Mitch put his head in his hands and started to sob. As Mary listened in horror, Mitch told her that Beau had been black mailing him. Beau found out that he had attached large fees to his private adoptions in Napa. He had asked Beau for advice on how to handle a young girl named Jolene who had changed her mind after delivering a healthy eight pound baby boy. Mitch had placed the child of the homeless girl with a wealthy family. The family had offered one hundred thousand dollars as a private adoption fee. They were told that the money would help the young mother go on to college. In fact, the young homeless girl signed away her parental rights and then changed her mind. Jolene's medical bills were paid but, the one hundred thousand dollars went right into Mitch's bank account. Mitch had contacted Beau when the girl came around and demanded to know about her child. Legally, the girl could change her mind. She was homeless but still wanted her child back. Beau sat in on their meeting one day. He generously offered the girl a job so that she could get on her feet, while they presumably tried to get her baby back.

Later that week, Beau told Mitch, "Jolene is no longer a problem." I asked, "Why?" Beau said, "These homeless kids often die on the street, so sad about Jolene." Mitch was dumb struck. Beau continued, "Why not consider moving your offices to Red Grape. Business is booming, and I need a backup on the city council. I can guarantee you fifty billable hours a month from the city." Mitch looked at his wife of twenty five years. Tears ran down her face, too, but something was gone. It was respect; she had lost her respect for him. Mitch loved his wife and she loved him, but he knew she would never look up to him again. He had been a party to murder, fraud, and a list of other crimes. "Why are you coming in at this time of night with claw marks on your face?" Mary asked. Mitch was still crying. "I could not do it." "What?" asked Mary. "Beau found out who has been writing those editorials in the *Grape Leaf*. He sent me to Kate Summers house to kill her tonight." Mary gasped, "Please tell me you did not murder that sweet old woman." Mitch went on, "No, I couldn't. It was all planned. I did break in. I went into her house, quietly walked upstairs, but when I approached her bed, I just stood there. And her damn cat attacked me like a demon, I have never seen a cat so huge!" "Thank God," said Mary. "Mitch, we have to call the sheriff. Maybe we can cut a deal if you agree to testify against Beau Geyser." "He is dangerous, Mary. He threatened to kill you if I did not follow through with this. He already killed John Marcel, the water expert." "Oh my God," said Mary. "I thought he had a heart attack." "Yea, a heart attack brought on by a drug mixed into his protein powder," Mary said calmly. "Mitch, pack an overnight bag and remember to pack your high blood pressure medication." Mary picked up the phone and dialed the Red Grape police department.

CHAPTER TWENTY-NINE

Rusty Returns to Red Grape

Rusty Waters had been in Napa talking to the Special Investigations Unit. He had just gotten back to town when he received an email from Helen. *Rusty, Anna is safe, Brad and I are at the sheriff's station. Talk later, Helen.* Rusty walked into the Chit Chat at about nine thirty and noticed Carol Marcel drinking martini's in a booth. Sally the bartender smiled and said, "Hello stranger," and served Rusty a Blue Moon. Leaning forward, Rusty said, "What in the hell is going on here tonight?" Sally grabbed the copy of the *Grape Leaf,* with the editorial titled, "*Who Can We Trust?*" By Stormy Day. When he finished the editorial, he said, "Hot damn, you folks run a rough town; there was less going on in Alaska." Sally laughed, "Looks like Beau Geyser may have finally been caught. Not sure what all the sirens have been about." When Rusty mentioned Beau Geyser, Carol Marcel looked up abruptly at the man at the bar. Carol grabbed her purse and put forty dollars on the table. She did not wait for change. She moved quickly toward the front door just as another police car from Napa raced down Main Street. The moon was full. The night was hot and dry. Carol had been so confident earlier in the evening. Her husband had left her everything including a large life insurance policy. Beau was not answering his phone, Carol felt very alone, and, very, very vulnerable.

CHAPTER THIRTY

A Respected Man

Beau Geyser had driven one town over to Vineland to the twenty four hour car wash. He had cleaned his car including the under carriage. He had also tried to contact Jordan Loggs, his media expert. He needed damage control. Jordan was not answering. Jordan had sent the text message. *Kate Summers is Stormy Day*. Beau had sent the message to McReady. All McReady had to do was put a pillow over the mouth of one old woman! What could go wrong? She lived alone. Another loose end, that little slut Anna had gotten away somehow. He had waited too long to silence her. His Hispanic workers had cleaned out her condo in less than an hour. Beau paid them cash and told them they could keep her things. Hell, she wouldn't be needing them. Anna knew no one in town, she was a foster child, and her one friend, Jolene, was dead. No loose ends! He drove home and went to bed. He would threaten a libel suit with *The Grape Leaf*, a good job for McReady. All would be well in the end.

CHAPTER THIRTY-ONE

Get Out of Town

At the airport in San Francisco, Jordan Loggs boarded the eight am flight for Bermuda. After all, lobbyists could work anywhere. It was time to get out of dodge for a while. Beau was going to take the fall for this disaster! Who knew the *Grape Leaf* publisher had a silent alarm system. Maybe Texas was a good place to start over.

CHAPTER THIRTY-TWO

The Sun Came Shining

A new day dawned in Red Grape. Sheriff Goodwin got into gear and used his San Francisco skills. He ran a back ground check on all parties involved in the previous night's wrongdoing. Beau Geyser's name came up with a prior. He had an arrest record for consorting with known prostitutes in San Francisco right before he moved to Red Grape in 2003. Phone records from Beau to Carol Marcel led the chief to a connection. Beau Geyser wanted John Marcel to change his report on fracking and water contamination. To assure that the preliminary report stayed buried, cortisol had been added to his protein powder. The Cortisol had been purchased on line by Carol Marcel. John Marcel was adding Cortisol to his protein drinks every day to better his health.

Maria Monroe had provided a statement regarding her job at the city offices. Her statement included the fact that Beau Geyser had directed her to clean John Marcel's office, remove the file on fracking, get rid of his computer and clean out his personal effects. She also produced the computer, which was still in the storage closet. Maria admitted to mailing John Marcel's water report to the *Grape Leaf*.

"I think you did a fine job last night, Bernie," said Sheriff Goodwin. "I don't believe anyone could have handled the situation better." "Hard to believe all of those emergencies came in at the same time," said Bernie. "Maybe our mayor was counting on us being hick cops out here in the sticks. I don't know, Andy, I have never been through anything like what happened last night." Andy laughed, "Pretty much a normal night for a city like San Francisco or Los Angeles." He said as he straightened the piles on his desk. "The tire treads on Beau Geyser's Beamer were a match on those dirt roads in front of St. Samuel's Vineyard. That places our mayor at the location where Anna escaped in Helen's car," said Bernie. "This morning, I took photos, of both the vineyard dirt road and of Beau's tires. Also, Beau's car had been washed last night and left on the street, which made it convenient to inspect." "Probably did not want to disturb his wife by opening the garage door so late," mumbled Andy, as he sipped his coffee. "Good work, Bernie. I don't want some slick lawyer saying those tracks were made at another time," he said.

"The city council meeting this week should be interesting," said Sheriff Goodwin. There may be a shortage of council members. Mc Ready is already arranging bail. Jordan Loggs bought a ticket for a flight to Bermuda, and seems to have left town. Beau Geyser will be in custody along with Carol Marcel by the end of the day. Anna is staying with Helen and Brad Elson. And, an officer had been on loan from Napa to watch Kate Summers house.

The two officers split the tasks of the day. Bernie was drafting five search warrants for the homes, and offices of all the men serving on the Red Grape City Council. Andy was requesting arrest warrants from the Napa District Attorney for Carol Marcel and Beau Geyser in connection with the murders of John Marcel and Jolene Perry. Mitch Mc Ready had come in and made a full confession of his involvement. Jolene Perry had been Mc Ready's client, and her strangulation was currently classified as the unsolved murder of a homeless woman in Napa. Jolene had been murdered in her camp site under a freeway in Napa almost a year ago. Mc Ready's confession included details of Beau Geyser's plot to poison John Marcel using powdered Cortisol mixed with his protein powder, with an assist from his wife Carol Marcel. Geyser's motive was greed. John Marcel had discovered that the ground water in Red Grape had been compromised by Sunshine Oil Corporation during a fracking incident. John had refused to modify his report. Headlines in tomorrow's paper would be on the Associated Press wire. By then, the whole nation would hear about the town of Red Grape and Andy's job as the sheriff in a quiet town might never be the same. The media would swarm into their small town. Well, maybe the publicity would help the locals. As usual, Andy was tuned to K-WIN and he turned up the volume for an old favorite; *This Land Is Our Land* by Woody Guthrie warbled out of the speakers. Andy sang along on his way down the highway. He pondered the events of recent months. In a big city or a small town, there is always greed and corruption. It can roll down Main Street or Wall Street alike. It happens in the Supreme Court and in small town city councils. But, this is our town and our country. Andy was satisfied that justice could still be found in America. As he sang along with Woody, Andy considered adopting a cat.

www.ingramcontent.com/pod-product-compliance
Lightning Source LLC
Chambersburg PA
CBHW020346260626
47156CB00004B/1693